Honey Moon

I0542364

# HONEY MOON

## ARLENE WEBB

Honey Moon
ISBN # 978-1-78430-784-4
©Copyright Arlene Webb 2015
Cover Art by Posh Gosh ©Copyright September 2015
Interior text design by Claire Siemaszkiewicz
Totally Bound Publishing

Published in 2015 by Totally Bound Publishing, Newland House, The Point, Weaver Road, Lincoln, LN6 3QN, United Kingdom.

Totally Bound Publishing is a subsidiary of Totally Entwined Group Limited.

# HONEY MOON

# Chapter One

His vision assaulted with vibrancy of dress — shapes and color — Sam worked his long frame down the walkway teeming with humanity. Agoraphobia not his deal, the occasional step on his heel or elbow to the side was nothing to raise blood pressure over. He loved to watch faces, more often seeing beauty and grace instead of conformity and ugliness. Young and old voices jabbered — talking into the wireless connection bubbled about their mouths and directly streaming to their wrist phones — while face-spacing with either an intimate, mini-hologram projection or going pictureless to chatter into the thin, congested air.

"Sorry, ma'am."

"Hey, watch it."

"Asshole. Move along."

"Yeah, baby, grab hold. I'm — wait, no — thief! Stop her!"

The most furious voice drew Sam's attention. The man ahead came to a halt, jarring the foot traffic moving toward the malls and the train lines, to stare at his arm. His bare arm. No wrist phone. The woman a few steps behind the victim stopped as well. Snarling at the people jostling on by with apathetic disrespect for the worldwide Good Samaritan code, she used her phone to snap pics of the young woman attempting to blend in with the group branching away from the shopping center toward the bullet trains.

Sam sighed and eased around an elderly couple to follow after the thief. People were ignorant and desperate. The vast criminal underbelly would snatch up a wrist phone, yes. But the thief would be lucky to get a week's rent in a cubicle shelter and maybe a couple of meals.

Odds were the woman who'd used one hand to grope a man, distracting him so she could slice the phone from his arm and hustle out of his reach, would be ID'd and tracked down within minutes of her picture pinging into World Security. Was stealing such a personal item worth five to twenty years behind bars?

Sam mentally shrugged. Based on the fact the victim still had two hands, at least the thief either hadn't used the latest switchblade to hit the streets or she was damn good. Micro-thin, the blade—known as the diamond-killer—could hide in the palm of a hand like an old-fashioned razor blade and cut through standard wristbands as if pliable metals were tissue paper.

He instinctively tucked his arm closer to his side, hand shoved in his pocket, and glanced at his own wrist phone. Made from inexpensive aluminum alloys processed under super high-pressure torsion, it was strong and incredibly lightweight but vulnerable to the latest weapons. It took a precise and controlled criminal to wield the diamond-killer, withdraw after just a nick through the band, kissing the skin to leave beads of blood but before the weapon chomped through muscle and bone. Hence the range of severity of penalty in this day and age of not if, but when, the perp was caught.

No matter the evolution of the human race, it seemed young and stupid remained constant. Too bad he, despite being in his mid-thirties, still clung to that juvenile mentality of thinking himself invincible, too clever and savvy to ever have his precious neck land on the chopping block. A terrible attitude when preparing to take on supreme forces that may or may not be evil.

Powerful lobbyists, groups of brilliant minds, rarely confronted the slightest infractions done by those behind the world governments, so what chance had a single idiot? Yet how could he pull someone else into his worries? He really should come up with a diabolical scheme that didn't involve a duo, but time wasn't on his side. If he was going to make a move, he had to stop dithering and set in motion the only idea he'd had to get a handle on his growing paranoia.

But what type of bastard seduces – then risks – the life of an innocent? Assuming he managed to bring a horrendous conspiracy into the light of day, it'd be highly unlikely he'd avoid the bullets the moment the prospective villains – either riding that free rocket ride with him or waiting on the moon – understood that he was the whistleblower.

*I don't know what else to do.* The deck was stacked one way or another, but with stakes this high, he couldn't live with himself if he didn't at least try. To quote a fictional hero from years past – 'The needs of the many outweigh the needs of the few'. Too bad he couldn't respond like a famous Vulcan and give the answer – 'or the needs of the one' — meaning it was only his bachelor ass on the line.

*I need to find a woman. ASAP. Get down on my knee within the month.*

Sam pressed on, angling his way to catch the train to take him to his new, one-room lair. Ten minutes of shallow breaths — glad colognes and perfumes were banned on the trains but geez, did someone really have to eat, say…cabbage soup before they went out in public? He happily disembarked.

His building was slotted in an endless row of the same. Sweat coated him by the time he reached the fourteenth floor. Should have taken an elevator, but at least the stairs belonged to him. Any of the elevators in this skyscraper would be packed worse than ants on a dropped ice cream, and he loved the exercise. He regretted reaching his level, causing yet another excuse to drag his heels on bringing the hunt for a fiancée to a close. He was about to embark on a quest from which there'd be little chance of turning back with his freedom, let alone his heart, intact.

He scanned his wrist phone to unlock the door and entered the eight by ten room. This hop online would most likely turn out to be the most asinine thing he'd ever done. He marched the three steps directly to the com-desk, sat and clicked on the icon linking him to what appeared to be a popular dating site.

*Christ, I should have done this a week ago.* Over a hundred million hopeful saps like him were trolling Arrow to the Heart in this moment. Eight thousand, one hundred and twelve and counting in his current city. Ever the optimist, he wondered, was it lame to think that maybe, just maybe, if he was honest and opened up, he'd find someone to do more than use? A sweetheart to love and cherish?

*Right. Then involve this sweetheart in the nuttiest of conspiracy theories.*

His fingers flew, tapping away on the flat desktop monitor. Took him three minutes to open a basic want-to-hook-up account. Two minutes too long, but the server was loaded with dreamers.

*Sigh. On to the personality profile.* Sam only had to lure someone into saying yes. He wasn't worried about winning the amazing newlywed lottos being offered, looks, money, or even finding instant love with the potential to endure the test of time. That'd be too much to ask. A woman with integrity, compassion and some balls? Not literally, but willing to take a huge risk for the greater good. Surely that was feasible?

He lied in the slots for name, employment and worth. Couldn't risk his true identity leaking out, let on to being a world-renowned bachelor. Admit his actual income, and he'd be overwhelmed with responses. Forget the literary world. He went with construction supervisor. On a planet so heavy with life, it took a stream of skilled engineers to upgrade buildings and homes. Architect was a job in consistent, strong demand. As to wealth, he allowed access to see the amount in one of his accounts, which labeled him as a basic good catch instead of a fairytale one.

More truthful in his next answers, he raced through the hundred yes, no, maybe questions rigged to gauge personalities, match like to like.

He gritted his teeth, raised his arm and took two selfies with his phone. Then he slapped out a couple of paragraphs of crap. *I – ha ha – love long walks on the beach. Never been – too crowded – but had to throw in that old cliché. Dancing in the rain – and who doesn't? Especially on non-acid Wednesday. And I'm definitely not a down-to-*

*Earth type guy, not with a honey of a moon shining above. I play hard, work harder… Wait, is that the other way round?*

*Seriously. I want someone I can trust and come to love to take my arm, sit beside me as we catch an out-of-this-world ride into whatever happy-ever-after we can win. Ping me. We'll chat.* Then he paid for two days of service and uploaded.

He stood and stripped off his shirt as he walked four feet to the shower cubicle. Five minutes later, towel around his waist, he opened the micro-fridge. Looked at both shelves, he saw nothing but an apple and a pretty much empty jar of multi-seed butter and closed it.

He flung himself down on the single bed and used his wrist phone to work his emails. He loved his job. Writing like he did, once or seven times a week, answering comments and getting off on the replies. He had thousands of 'friends' who occasionally gave him their thoughts on his ponderings, but a handful of commentators in particular made his heart jump when he saw they'd messaged.

Sam didn't know or care if JJ was a man or a woman, gay, bi or straight. He loved how he-she pushed buttons. No comment today as of yet. He sighed, answered the most pressing messages then peeked at the logo for the dating site.

*Holy crap.* His breath caught. The number 216 rode on the red arrow. That many matches? *Bloody hell, I'm a dating site stud?* He sat back down at the com-desk. These women, unless they lied and he couldn't think of a single reason why they would, had a home in his corner of the city, placing them within a short bullet train ride.

He squared his shoulders and started alphabetically. Abigail, Amber, Amy, Arwen — all sounded wonderful.

He barely glanced at their pics, homing in on dreams and desires.

Thirty replies, some short and sweet, others longer and more intense, to thirty randomly selected women, and he hit send simultaneously.

A half hour later, and *oh yeah*, he had thirty replies and forty new enquiries. Life would be good if he was an honest Romeo instead of a scheming Casanova who pretty much loved everyone indiscriminately. In general, he found people to be awesome—fascinating and special, even when first glance or first words exchanged were mundane. All these sweet women looking for adventure and escape… He couldn't help but yearn to wrap his arms around each. Wish them the best of luck in finding a real prince.

He gritted his teeth, and zeroed in on weeding out those with any hint of closet or blatant bigotry in their profiles. In the interest of survival, humans had a selfish gene. In some, the need to reproduce with the best of the best, to attain social status no matter the cost, lay more dormant than in others. Seeing as he wasn't about finding a mate to bear the perfect child or to help him forge ahead of the monetary pack, he only needed a partner who had either a strong moral compass or a death wish. Forgetting any of the standard questions to help pinpoint a sociopath—a ruthless personality that may actually be an asset when confronting the equivalent of Goliath—he focused on intolerance issues. Then he picked the women who'd also answered that they loved poetry in their profile, scrubbed the weariness from his eyes and shrugged at how lame he was presenting himself.

*If you met a man from Nantucket whose #### was so long he could suck it, would you care if he only shared with a guy named Bucket?*

*If our daughter was in love with a gal from Nantucket who kept all her cash in a bucket, would you rather see her run away with the XY who took it?*

*If you bumped into a prick from Nantucket, who only dipped in the same gender bucket...*

He worked the questions around standard answers concerning cat or dog, porn or reality — yada and yada — and copied and pasted to one cutie after the other.

After a few hours of sleep, he'd not bothered reading past the first few replies. Just pick and get on with the charming. He set his wrist phone, his head hit the pillow, and faces flashed across his shut eyelids. *Beautiful, sweet, gentle loves, which of you wants to play terrorist with me?*

* * * *

The ding and low-voltage zap of his alarm shook him out of a deep sleep. He blinked, found his feet then dropped his butt in the com-chair.

*Oh no, no, no.* What'd he do? So what that he'd never been to a dating site before. How could he have screwed up this royally? Just had to put those dumbass rhyming questions in. Unreal. Out of hundreds of spectacular choices, only four potential love interests hadn't closed out of further contact.

Lisa: *Yes, my handsome male, I love to #### Man-tucket. I used to have a #### as long as all that, so cum sit on my bucket...*

On to the next...

Tracy: *If there's a man who lies with a male, surely he shall be put to death…*

Gulp.

Kim: *I don't understand poetry. But your –* she means you're *– cute. Want to met –* sigh, meet *– me? No one else answers me.*

Poor dear.

Laree: *Ha ha, you're funny. I'm going to ignore the silly questions. All you need to know before we have a face-to-face is that you made my list of top hundred. Seeing as I crush any competition, I expect you'll meet me at Spenders tomorrow night at 5 p.m.*

No typos, plenty of arrogance and expensive taste for Ms. Laree. His wallet ached just thinking about the most upscale club in the city. He'd need a decent suit, a trendy tie and a hundred bucks for two drinks at the bar, let alone greasing palms to get a dinner reservation that would set the average Joe back a week's salary, even when gender equality was the norm and dates usually split the bill. Based on numerous pictures, Laree was gorgeous – her killer smile and designer clothing said she was accustomed to a silver spoon. And yep, she'd picked that the best era to live was a couple of hundred years ago. Either she wasn't smart enough to know it gave away that she liked the time period when men were expected to open every door, pay each bill, never let her step in mud let alone worse – or she didn't care.

He'd answered that he thought the current time period was fantastic, the future exciting and if he got teleported into a steampunk romance, he hoped travel would be within the Milky Way or beyond, but in the present or the future. So what did a woman draped in faux furs and glittery jewelry want with him then? The obvious answer? She was broke and wanted a free ride on a respectable man's arm. Not much choice now that he'd blown it with close to three hundred others.

His gut churning, feeling the fool, the last thing he wanted to do was mess with this site any further or start another. No doubt he'd get on bended knee to a transgender, a homophobe, a simpleton or a privileged princess.

*Whatever will be is gonna be screwed if I'm involved.* He wilted, laying his head down on the com-desk.

\* \* \* \*

*Oh wow.* Jenna shot her palm beneath her chin to keep from head-banging her com-desk. Over three dozen victims complaining of problems with dating sites in the past few days? *Crap piled high.* How many hopeful singles would—or did—get reeled in by dishonest means?

Jenna sighed, wishing for the umpteenth time that she'd taken any job other than drone for a viral support group. Mostly the only help she could give was to connect victims with others who'd fallen prey to the same scam.

On the WG—World Governments—site for the North America Continent, she saw a disclaimer that had been posted yesterday. It stated that all 'love-bugs' would be eradicated within forty-eight hours. According to WG, this bug they'd labeled IDS—Infect-Delete-Score—fell into the category of soft crimes, seeing as monies weren't exchanged between the con and their mark, and they weren't responsible for policing such.

Jenna skimmed the details, coming to understand losers wanting to hook up without effort and willing to spend a hefty amount to do so, had paid for the viral code on some site that was up for a matter of hours then gone. They zeroed in on a hot prospect—good-looking and wealthy—and buggered the account so he or she lost most, if not all, of their matches and were blocked from new ones. Then if the victim remained unaware that their account they hadn't bothered to protect with more than simplistic firewalling was hacked, they'd chat with the few matches left, unaware they were dealing with some cheater.

Jenna drew a deep breath and turned toward the mini-cubicle to her left. "Hey, Lib? You get any messages from vics on dating sites about some new IDS bug?"

Lib's dark head popped up, peering down at her. "Yeah, hon, I did. I'm swamped with a medical scam, so I forwarded to you."

"Whaaat?"

Lib grinned, raised her hand and flashed her ring finger, sporting a sparkly band of studded silver and gold. "I'm engaged, sweetie. You aren't."

Jenna couldn't scowl any deeper. "Nice. Because I haven't trolled for Mr. Right on a dating site, haven't fallen prey to Mr. Wrong with a tiny dong who'd rather cheat than face competition, I have time to handle this? The messenger who gets bitched at if I explain the person they're in bed with—making plans to walk down an aisle with—is most likely an asshole who paid thousands for a tricky bug that overwhelmed dating sites have yet to completely squash?"

Lib beamed. "Glad you understand."

Jenna raised her ringless hand with middle finger extended. Lib laughed and plopped back down.

Her head swam. There was much on her radar and so little time. On the off chance the least of worries for new lovers was how they'd met, Jenna slapped all the IDS messages into a folder with the icon of Superwoman in a cape with hands on hips and a bubble from her mouth saying the procrastination meeting had been postponed.

# Chapter Two

"Yes," Laree said. "As long as we get a better home. A humongous one."

On bended knee, Sam smiled up at the most materialistic woman he'd ever met in his life, let alone the past month — and the dumbest. With the population on Earth exceeding eighteen billion and no wars in the past five decades to kill off the young and fertile, only an elite few owned a home larger than a prison cell.

The opportunist he could now call his fiancée had seen the videos and heard about mansions spreading like a swarm of locusts on a terraformed Mars. After weeks of clandestine research before he'd been idiotic enough to troll for a bride to use, he'd concluded that the pictures and propaganda posted by the world's largest marriage broker couldn't be genuine. He worried that for better or worse — through deceit or true love — the bit about 'until death us do part' could well happen much sooner than any phony or real lovebirds imagined.

Or not. Could be he was certifiably stupid in his paranoia. Sam's jaw twitched, his stomach in knots because he'd rather hoped she'd have said no. Not easy, but he maintained the false persona of a happy man, the sparkle in his gaze and smile wide, watching as Laree admired the ring.

Current happenings were intense, shaping history in ways no one could have dreamed possible a mere few months ago. Hundreds of first-time shuttles prepared to launch in a week and that meant millions of guys were on their knees and under the gun. Jewelry stores competed fiercely for soaring sales as couples rushed to file applications and get married in time to hopefully score big time—all with dreams of winning either the round trip vacation to the moon or the one-way tickets to travel onward and be a part of booming colonies on the outer planets.

He'd gotten a look at protected, top secret schematics of aircraft designed to travel beyond the low orbit of Earth, then continue roughly 384,400 kilometers to land on the moon—a surface without an atmosphere—and return without refueling. Equipped with orbiters and external tanks, four solid rocket boosters with a million pounds of super-charged liquid propellants in each, six main engines per—these shuttles had to each carry a price tag of a couple of billion dollars.

He hadn't been able to get copies of working blueprints for functional shuttles, but the problem was he shouldn't have been able to access the prototype schematics. The paranoid mindset would think they'd been planted to lull the suspicious person searching for a hoax. But regardless of the seemingly legit set-up, he was a firm believer in the fact that free rides don't exist on Earth or to its satellite. That suckers were still being born every minute, despite powerful population controls, and the entire free honeymoon and home project was highly suspect.

By the way Laree peered at the glimmering stone he held out to her, it looked as if little Miss Gold-Digger harbored doubts of her own. The predatory heat in her eyes told him they didn't concern the Love Center, also known as the LC, but the con man in front of her.

She snatched the ring from him. "Is this real?"

Yes. No contaminated carbon. Pure and shiny, it had cost a fortune. He sighed. "Of course."

Her narrowed gaze told him she'd get the rock appraised at first chance. *Greedy young lady, but she expects that I love her.* Ripples of guilt danced down his spine. A good man would come clean. Try to get her onboard, literally, but with eyes wide open.

Unfortunately, he couldn't get past his gut instinct to trust that she'd err on the side of the greater good, just too eager to join her peers doing whatever it took to avoid being a bridesmaid left on Earth. She'd pursued him aggressively once she saw he met her expectations of attractiveness and had a decent amount in the bank. He'd made a big mistake. Should have ended it on the first date, but he'd hoped that getting to know her better would prove him wrong about both her and the LC.

Now it was too late to walk away. If he spilled the truth to Laree, she'd either dump him or turn him in as a potential terrorist expecting that the LC would reward her with a lot more than marriage and a free ride into space.

Laree jammed the diamond on her finger, and held her hand up to catch the light. "Pretty. For now. Get up, Samuel. I've everything planned — dress, tuxedo, new luggage. You need to send off payments."

He slumped. He'd played the role of an infatuated shmuck, but seriously? How could any bride be this shallow and not give the groom more part in a life's milestone, other than footing the bill? He pushed to his feet, his goofy smile in place. "Will do, babe. You've made me the happiest guy alive."

His heart thumped painfully. The end part of that—alive—was accurate, but logic said not for long. Odds were he'd stop breathing within days of her demands and extravagances emptying out the bank account he'd given her access to. After he crossed his fingers behind his back and said 'I do', there'd be no rocket into the sunset that'd end well for him.

The most optimistic scenario? He'd survive a lunar landing and begin divorce proceedings only to be gutted, stabbed in the back by his money-hungry bride upon learning that he was a famous multimillionaire who had fallen for a conspiracy that didn't exist and trolled her into it.

There was the chance his lover would also be dead before the honeymoon started, if Laree figured out who he really was and ratted him out to the LC. Could be the corporation would rather see her have an accident than pay her off. He should be ecstatic she'd yet to see beyond the sparkly bauble to the impostor in front of her. Long blonde tresses, legs that didn't know how to end and a curvaceous figure guaranteed she'd snag a real hubby, if only she survived his treachery.

Laree snorted. "Get up, darling, and come sign where I tell you. I won't settle for any honeymoon other than the moon."

"Then the moon it shall be." He stood and gestured her to the com-desk.

She walked across the cramped bedroom. "We must get top marks."

"Understood." He had the application memorized and was certain, assuming his bride-to-be didn't screw things up, they'd score the deadly jackpot.

Laree sat down in the only chair. "Anna, a brain surgeon in her prime, didn't qualify. But that slut Denise who dances in a strip club won a condo — Mars or some satellite of Jupiter." Her slender fingers danced, tapping angrily on the touch screen com-desk. "Do you think the LC's corrupt? Takes bribes?" She angled in the seat to peer at him. "How much are you willing to offer them?"

He winked at her. "Whatever it takes. On second thought, why don't you go hop in the shower? I'll handle this then join you. Okay, my love?" *Babe, angel, my love — how many inane endearments can I cram into two minutes?*

"I'm not sharing that dinky little bathroom with you ever again," Laree grumbled. "And no, I don't trust you with something this important." She returned her attention to the screen. "It doesn't seem right so many losers I know won a paid honeymoon *and* a free, three-story manor on Mars or a Jupiter satellite."

*Bingo.* Vacationing in upscale resorts within massive domes welded onto lunar rock sure looked fantastic online. Shopping malls that stretched on and on, golf courses where a ball could travel as far as a man could hit, spacious hotel rooms that'd easily fit a three or foursome in the shower with only the right spots getting banged — pretty much anything a couple could want on an out-of-this-world getaway.

The catch? According to the Love Center there was but one. If you won the fab trip to the moon, you'd be incommunicado with Earth, unless you could afford a mere ten thousand, five hundred dollars for twenty seconds of email privileges, payable in advance in increments of ten seconds, with a minimum of a minute and yep, that included time lag if others jammed the server at the same time. He suspected they'd not offer face-time as well as messaging, meaning that someone could be sitting anywhere on Earth to intercept the message and pretend to be anyone, such as a loving relative.

The other, more insidious condition—which the LC didn't broadcast—was that they practiced discrimination. All of the couples who rated high enough on the application to secure a seat on the shuttles fit a specific profile. His Intel showed that healthy heterosexuals or bisexuals, personalities with aggressive, materialistic interests, consistently won at least the free honeymoon. No sick, gays, or 'don't care if you live in a closet-sizes space on an overcrowded planet' allowed. He chuckled at the irony.

"What's so funny? Pay attention and write what I say, you doofus," Laree said. "Think I'd marry a loser?"

*No. Just sleep with one, despite no chemistry, just casual sex.* "Yes, dear, and no, dear. The questionnaire won't take long. Whereas I, massaging your gorgeous body in the shower, will require at least a half hour or so, right?"

She didn't answer. He scowled. The tip of her tongue between her lips and, he imagined, visions of white gowns dancing in her head, Laree concentrated on the screen.

*Stop stalling and embrace your doom.* He walked the three feet to the desk, grasped her shoulders and examined the page centered on the acrylic desktop monitor with the Love Center logo across the top. Two gleaming gold and diamond bands shaped like hearts bounced toward each other, coming together to interlink with a capital L and C as they rolled across a silver full moon. The same emotion gripped him every time he saw the damn symbol—the urge to howl and smash his fist on it. He forced himself to unclench his fingers and direct his gaze to the questionnaire.

Not good. Glaring problems already. *Jackass.* Had he wasted a month seducing this woman? It was time to throw the lady aside and claim the com-chair. Gambling with so many lives required him to function without any margin for error.

He tightened his grip on her. "That program records how often you change answers. Stop touching the screen and let me fill that out." *Before I break those manicured fingers.*

"I know what I'm doing," Laree snapped.

"World-renowned shrinks formulated those questions. The answer for number five won't win us seats."

Her jaw sagged. "But I hate kids."

"Saying you've thought about it doesn't mean you plan to be a parent." *And never with me as the sperm donor.* He made damn sure he used the foolproof condoms the government issued for free. Not any of the vibrating, drug-saturated, gimmicky ones offered on the black market for a price and a .009 percent slip-off-the-dick chance.

She jerked against his hold. "I'm not stupid."

*Right.* "This questionnaire uses reverse psychology." His voice tone patient, regret churned in his stomach as he released her. *I'll never hear a little voice call me Daddy.* "Most women want children. If you say not ever, not even as a possibility in the distant future, it tags you as a liar."

"Oh."

"Same concept for number eight," he said. "Change your answer saying the government shouldn't be allowed to dictate progeny based on income. Yes to a GSA is good. Claiming you'd get a government-sponsored abortion shows you understand population

control is a critical issue." And by marking no for GSS —
government-sponsored sterilization — it tipped them
off that she could well skip the birth control at some
point. "Most importantly, no way do we agree to any
archaic snipping of nuts." Why bother? Not like he'd
impregnate anyone if he was either dead or in prison.

She glowered at him. "I want — I *deserve* a nice home,
and what I do *not* want is a child, so who turns down a
free vasectomy? It's simple, darling. I think they
reward the pairs who won't contribute to the start of
overpopulation on other worlds."

*Wrong.* They gathered the couples most likely to
breed. He couldn't understand any reason for excluding
gays and sterilized heterosexuals other than a
diabolical one.

"There is no way I can afford this," he murmured.
"Either we win or we honeymoon here on Earth in
grimy Las Vegas. You want the bloody moon? Stop
arguing and trust me."

She glanced at his groin, inches from her face. "Trust
you'll never have my mouth on..."

He tuned her out and shoved her fingers away from
the com. The thought of the BJs he'd be forced to give a
three hundred pound cellmate before he was executed
had his cock shriveled and his hands shaking.

Shortly, he'd have more evidence supporting his
theory that lower income heteros who admitted to
wanting at least one child automatically won a
luxurious honeymoon, or he'd learn he'd best grab a
tinfoil hat and join the spouting paranoid-crap club. He
finished the questionnaire and stood so his lovely
fiancée had full view of the com-screen.

"Okay, yeah, I guess this looks good," she muttered,
as he stepped to stare blankly out of the window into a
dusty gray-blue sky.

He couldn't wrap his head around this marriage broker not only creating a quadrillion dollar infrastructure on the barely colonized moon, but that they had all these shuttle-rockets strategically placed around Earth, ready to transport newlyweds wanting to celebrate nuptials on the moon. Then, the crème de la crème on an already unbelievable package? Each passenger was entered into a lotto where winners were handed deeds to property on the outer planets.

Comfortable living in the Milky Way was plausible. Eons after the sound barrier was broken by an object made of matter, the difficulties of cracking the speed of light barrier had burst. Figuring out how an object could travel faster than the electromagnetic fields linking its atoms — moving a rocket at the speed of light by adding infinity energy — was credited to a pair of siblings.

The real miracle was the fact that the brother and sister hadn't been aborted. If the mom hadn't stayed off the grid, avoided healthcare, the first prenatal chromosome scan would have shown the fetuses with gross defects. The twins lacked functional synapses in alternate sides of their brains. The parents hid their existence until the eight-year-olds got themselves published in science journals with articles on tachyons, wormholes, space-time warping with the negative implications of creating time paradoxes being redundant.

In the simplistic terms he understood, they'd shown a doable means to draw IE — infinite energy — from a vacuum and utilize it within a spaceship. That in turn provided the power needed to alter time by speeding through time-space. He'd read the publications, got the gist of maybe one percent of the math, and been thrilled to imagine the possibilities of colonizing space in his lifetime.

The past decade had also seen tremendous advances in technology, including mass-production of sheets of graphene. They'd developed carbon nanotubes able to retain their ultralight and strongest alloy in existence properties, even when stitched together.

Affiliates of the LC claimed to have successfully colonized planets on a massive scale. Homes and gardens built inside translucent domes were made out of this newfangled super-graphene alloys and supposedly tested with consistent results showing the terrarium-style enclosures could withstand extreme temperatures and pummeling by massive meteoroids, even comet collisions.

It was an amazing era to be alive.

And a terrible one to have a life cut short.

If only he had a solid grasp of evil intent—but no. Circling the bleeding neurons that made up his mind, he had little but fears that'd started out as minnows named WTF, then morphed into giant sharks who answered to Martyr, Masochist, Attention-Seeker and so on. Meanwhile, the question of why he didn't go public—let the authorities sort it out—got pushed farther and farther into the abyss of no return.

He sighed as he stared out over the neon-lit city, so thick with SHIT—what the locals called the buildings, based on the acronym of the slogan *Scraping Heaven is Tangible*, dreamed up by some marketing idiot—he couldn't tell if the dull sparks in the gray sky were stars or beacons marking the pinnacles.

Suspecting without proof—other than bigotry toward gays and guys with documented vasectomy points— the nefarious nature of the homes on offer was one thing. Creating an elaborate ruse in hope of exposing a powerful monopoly with ties to every government on Earth was quite another. Not like he was police, licensed journalist or had a family member duped into whatever this was or wasn't.

Sam was nothing but a general do-gooder with a popular political blog, about to get his ass handed to him. A guy who couldn't sleep at night thinking of the potential body count, and he was afraid to squeal before he had something more tangible than projection based on illegally-gotten statistical spreadsheets. Without the public behind him, it'd be simple to frame him as a nutjob, then make him disappear. Ergo, the need for a bride. The ruse of a guy who took advantage of a woman, dreams of status and power in her eyes and not a bit of love, but still an innocent, so he could get onto a shuttle and see without rose-tinted glasses what — if anything — was rotten.

Then the reply came. Samuel Cooper and Laree Gilson had a day to file the thousand dollar marriage certificate confirming their seats on shuttle 7877 leaving in one week.

The yippee and big kiss Laree gave him were delightful.

The huge black hole of insecurity rolling in his gut? Not so much.

\* \* \* \*

Two days later, Laree seized Sam's wrist phone off the desk and read the mysterious text — *Congratulations. A wedding gift awaits. Wear a red rose. Be there tomorrow — 3p.m. — or suffer a terrible consequence.* It included an address for what had to be a bar.

"Damn it, Laree. Don't answer that. Leave it to me." He grabbed it from her and slapped the band around his wrist. "You need to order my tux and email everyone we'll be off the grid for a month. Six months or longer if we hit the jackpot with that home you want on Europa. Only the biggest and the best for my girl."

*I'm such a bastard.* If he was wrong or failed to show the world the truth, there was a slight possibility his bride would get a five-by-five cell, regardless of the vid-cam and un-posted blog he'd left hidden on his server, documenting that any subversive acts were his and his alone.

Laree arched her brows. "Whoever sent that text blocked their ID. I thought that was a crime?

Also, wanting to give a wedding gift in person at some tavern I've never heard of, instead of using the Net? It's so creepy."

And damn expensive. A black market wrist phone with ID blocked had to be incinerated within a time window he imagined to be less than a few hours or the user could be tracked.

"If you think I'm a sucker who'll fall for a bachelor prank, why don't you meet me there?"

She laughed. "You know what happens in old-fashioned bars?"

"People have a drink?"

"People are exposed as losers. Only lowlifes go to dumps that aren't clubs."

Right. Pay exorbitant cover charges for an overpriced, watered-down drink. Perhaps the sender had more concern for his wallet. The cryptic text gnawed at him.

The moment Laree sat at the desk, he typed on his wrist phone – *Terrible consequence if I turn down this wedding present? K. 2pm, not 3.*

He'd find out if someone was onto him before Laree arrived, then he'd whine to her that no one had shown and waste another minute trying to coax her into at least letting him finish his cheap beer before she dragged him out the door with her nose held high.

\* \* \* \*

The next morning, he was back at the bedroom window and watching the sun climb the horizon against a cloudless backdrop, brightening the perpetual smog hazing the city. Millions of humans surrounded him in this metropolis alone, so why did he feel like the most isolated nutter on Earth?

He angled the blind, encouraging rays to penetrate the solitary window of their sixty-third floor abode. The light kissed Laree in the face, causing her to blink, and he slid back into bed. He eased his arm over to rest his hand on her hip.

She groaned. "Samuel, please. Get your hand off my ass, close that damn shade and be a dear. I need breakfast."

*Yeah, yeah.* He hopped out of bed.

The lonely jitterbugs prowling within him died painfully, stamped out by self-pity as he dumped cereal into a bowl and hunted unsuccessfully for milk. Not even a cuddle to start one of the last days he had left as a free man on this beautiful planet, then nothing to eat but multigrain flakes. Laree was obsessed with not leaving a crumb for a cockroach before hopping the cruise rocket heading to a gluttonous holiday on the moon and beyond.

He cracked open the carton of OJ, sniffed and waited. When he didn't keel over dead from past expiration dated fumes, he poured juice over the cereal while walking from the kitchen into the partitioned bedroom slash office.

"Whaaat?" He set the bowl on the desk beside Laree's elbow. She'd looked at his offering with a flinch. He shrugged and raised the orange juice carton. He drank, head tipped back, to hide from the annoyance gathering in her eyes.

"Wipe your mouth, go shave and get out of here, darling. Be sure you're back in time."

He dutifully wiped his mouth and offered her the carton. "Go where and back in time for what?"

She slammed the juice down onto the desk, blew a heavy sigh and he braced.

"We went over this yesterday. You need to return that tux. Make them lower the pant cuffs. I told them you were six foot four, but did they listen? Then run this list of errands before meeting me at that bar."

*Onward bachelor soldier, marching as to war...*

* * * *

Sam left the tux at the tailor, jogged shoulder to shoulder with strangers in Central Park, sat on a concrete bench and people watched.

At 1 p.m. he boarded the automated train, got off a few blocks from a florist shop, then hopped onto the southbound train.

One forty-five p.m., carrying the requested rose instead of wearing the thing, Sam tromped down the block toward the establishment called Fill That Hole. *Mouth, heart, butt? Hmm, the bride will say the biggest hole is where my soul should be.*

Nestled between a drugstore and an office building, the squat bar claimed a good-sized lot that included a filled parking area. His check on the Net had informed him the owners were fighting and losing against a city ordinance to tear down the historic building and clear space for another skyscraper. He enjoyed a brief feel of grass clinging to his boots, the rough crunch of gravel as he closed in to push open the door.

The gritty stench of illegal tobacco, mixed with legal weed, wafted from dark corners. About twenty people sat at the long bar. The quaint pool tables in the back had groups clustered around them as well.

Two cool mouthfuls of hops and barley later, a timid throat clearing had him swiveling the barstool.

*Yowsa.* Bouncy reddish-brown curls, adorable splash of freckles across her cheeks and a rosebud mouth begging to be kissed, if only to ease away the nervous quiver. Soft scents of fresh lemon and crisp cinnamon. Mid-twenties. No makeup. Black skirt, buttoned blouse and honest-to-Christ sneakers, instead of stilettos. Not the usual trolling-for-cash get-up. Neither was she the clichéd version of a call girl. Skinny and too short—about perfect for a condemned groom.

"Samuel Cooper?"

*She's my gift? Please, please, please.* "Who's asking?"

The woman glanced at the wilted rose lying beside his hand. "In private." Blood as bright as the flower flooded her cheeks as she mumbled, "Follow me."

Who'd have purchased an escort? One who seemed as naïve and uncomfortable as if she reeled in her first john?

The pretty lady dipped her chin, muttering, "If you want to live—come," and walked away.

*"Come? Seriously?" asked dick.*

*"We're saying 'I do' in two days, numbnuts," scolded brain. "Gotta be a trap."*

*Ahh, hell.* He slugged down another mouthful of the beer, scanned his wrist phone for payment and went after a sweetly curved—*gulp*—into the washroom.

His fingers moved without thought to slide the deadbolt locking the door to the deserted room, while he scanned the area. Three stalls, each larger than his apartment. He knocked the swing door open to the last, closed it behind him and eyeballed the beauty staring at him with so much trepidation in her gaze that his dick slumped along with his heart. This woman wasn't a hooker — not a doubt in his mind.

# Chapter Three

One thing Jenna Jensen was sure of, no man should have eyes that green, a mop of thick, dark hair and such a lean, yet muscular, body that went up and up—over a foot taller. She suspected it'd only take a tap on top of her crazy head to bang her knees to the floor.

She swallowed hard, fumbled in the front pocket of her skirt and yanked out the miniature, but concentrated, weapon. "Pepper spray," she squeaked, pointing the tiny vial at him.

Mister Too-damn-gorgeous-not-to-be-trouble, a.k.a. Samuel Cooper, raised his palms up and out. His forehead furrowed. "Ah, lady of the...afternoon, get real. You're the one who lured me here."

*That I did.* Hypnotized by emerald eyes and the confident timbre of his voice, she swallowed hard and hesitantly shoved the spray back in her pocket.

"I won't hurt you. I promise." He lowered his hands and her attention went south with them. "What's this all about?"

*Do not. Do not stop to ogle at Pleasure Island.* She jerked her gaze past his waist to his feet. "An anonymous friend of yours…um…paid for…this."

His black, buffed boots stayed rooted to the floor and relief swelled her lungs. So far intelligent confusion seemed to control his Id, instead of opportunistic caveman. Once she got past the stammering dolt stage, perhaps she'd survive this encounter unscathed.

"Huh," his low voice rasped. "Then I'm damn grateful to someone. Is there a limit on what *this* involves?"

She didn't dare raise her chin. "I'm to do whatever you want, but I'm really here to warn—I mean, I should explain some facts. Privacy laws aren't always enforced. That's common knowledge, so a man about to get married must be careful. I get extra if we don't cause any undue attention. Please try to understand. I don't want anything at all to happen, no contact… That is, not above a whisper." *In other words, beating me bloody or screwing me in any way is out of the question.*

"So I'm clear, you've been hired to…service me—quietly?"

"Yes." *Get to it. Mumble onward.* "Low voices mean surveillance videos won't be activated."

GI—Governments, Inc.—monitored and recorded everything worldwide, making 'this' a problem if she needed to spell it out further. Certainly even the average bloke knew that rough voices, cries of passion or pain, and—*shiver*—conspirators plotting too loudly, got routed to monitors being manned by bored agents. They'd have a look and a listen, and decide if they should boost the feed to pick up every whisper within a mile radius of her rapidly-beating heart.

Those big boots shifted uneasily, but stayed in place. "You're saying I can do whatever in the privacy of this stall," Cooper said, "including my hand covering your mouth, as long as there's no audible screaming. Does the afternoon delight include multiples — or is it wham-bam?"

"What?" *Wait, hand over mouth? God no, not again.* She cringed and slapped her hand on her pocket, feeling the pepper spray.

"Is there a time limit?" he asked in a dry voice.

Perhaps he too was nervous. Was it odd she found that slightly comforting, but still couldn't seem to face him? "Of course. Fifteen... Ten minutes and counting."

Dark blue, two-by-two square tiles, white grout. At least the floor she may soon be pressed against looked as well-polished as it did the last time — no sign of blood, spit or other fluids.

"Then I'll unwrap such a beautiful gift quickly."

His voice had hardened. A glob of fear slid down her throat as he continued. "My preference includes a demand. If you can't look me in the eye, see me for the man that I am, then don't speak any further."

*See him for who he is? Like I should recognize him?* She lifted her chin. Her eyes widened at the lack of aggression and flash of empathy in his expression. Any thought she might already know him scattered, as she tumbled into flecks of hazel becoming darker and darker shades of green.

She flinched back as he leaned for her ear without touching her.

"Stop that," he muttered "and leave the damn spray alone. Nervous isn't good when posing as a professional. I suspect there's two cams, the door and behind you. Make sure you whisper when I allow and sorry, but it's also common knowledge an escort isn't paid to use their mouth for chit-chat. Forgive me."

"Forgive you?" She gulped, staring at his chest. "Listen. There's something... Another gift that you won—"

"Never mind," he snapped. "I told you to either look at me or shut up. I'll help with that." He grasped her by the throat, jerked her head back and his lips took hers.

*Lack of aggression? I'm so wrong. He's a wolf. Help! Stop! No, don't. Wow...yessss.*

His firm lips pressed, molded and shaped hers, and her legs turned to mush as he gave her little choice— either submit or risk the hand slipping beneath her hair to gently clasp the back of her head, then twisting to crack her skull against the wall.

He grew more insistent. *What's wrong with me?* Her lips parted, his tongue shot in and she gasped at the instant current racing along her spine. He swallowed her moan and without pause, his kiss galloped past fairytale, beyond sweet romance, heading toward erotic sci-fi bestseller.

*Why am I so attracted to this stranger?* Yin to yang. Iron to magnet. Double hydrogen to oxygen... *Who the hell is he?* She found her arms clutching his waist, gluing herself to him as if he was the key to a gaping hole within her. *Who the hell am I?*

A hint of foamy beer, testosterone rising, a cascade of sex in her mouth with delicious lips promising he had so much more to give. In and out, his tongue explored and plundered in a skilled yet relentless, escalating rhythm. Every nerve she had hummed with a sizzling desire for faster, harder, more. Moisture pooled between her legs and her lungs remained locked. Who needed oxygen? Why breathe if sucking air instead of him would interrupt a missile headed toward fireworks?

Her brain fogged even further as it registered his other hand no longer rested on her hip, but inched her skirt upward. Her body reacted without her say-so. She pushed backward, granting him easier access and—*nooo*—he eased free from the hottest kiss of her life.

He didn't move those lips far. She panted, her temperature rocketing into supernova territory. He nuzzled her neck, nibbling the pounding blood trying to jerk out of her skin. "Who are you?" he murmured. "What do you want? Explain fast, or you'll have to pardon me for more than just a kiss."

*Just a kiss? Is he nuts? I'm speechless. Marked. Nothing, no man will ever taste the same.*

He tugged her back, his lower body firm against her. His hold tightened as he understood she could easily melt into a puddle at his feet—not that that would be a bad thing. Reduced to nothing but drops of lust, she'd trail down his chest, a clinging waterfall of need, tasting his groin, dripping along his cock and down those long legs—*concentrate, you idiot. What'd he say?*

Pardon him for more than a kiss? He'd spoken quietly but clearly and without a hint of indecision. An alpha promising he'd be too fast and powerful to manipulate. The barn door was open and *ohmygodohmygod.* Long, thick and hard pressed into her stomach. "I-I… What?"

He chuckled as he lowered his lips back to her ear. "You forgot your name?" His low tones were barely audible. Warm breath sent rushes of heat careening throughout her. "Doesn't matter—and good you don't know me. My identity would trigger unwanted interest. I'm hoping the feeds don't transmit farther than the vault of who cares. Say no if I go too far. And yes, damn it, your knee will work as well. Now ask me what I want in a normal tone."

He pulled back, dark gaze staring at her, and she pushed the words out, "I'm sterile. Certified clean. Your preference?"

"Upfront fuck. Clothes on," he said in a soft voice, but clear enough for low-budget security. "No more discussion, except I'll pay as well if you whisper the dirtiest words you know."

Excitement and horror danced in her stomach. She'd never had consensual sex with a stranger before, let alone on camera in a public restroom.

He splayed his fingers across her lower back as he bent to her ear. "Speak to me so audio can't pick up. Please. Hurry before I forget this is an act. Sorry. You're so sweet, pretty and...er...fuckable." His other hand tightened on her hip, the skirt draped over his arm and her black panties exposed. Her legs trembled, nerves on fire as his fingers crept for the elastic band.

Jenna closed her eyes. "You gotta trust me," she whispered. "I'm not crazy, just read between lines, do the math and reach conclusions. I worry if you" — a ray of thought poked through the lust cloud. This man intimately caressing along the rim of her panties was about to get married — "and your fiancée get on one of those lunar shuttles leaving in two days that you'll not walk on any satellite or anywhere for long."

His hand stilled, perilously close to pushing her into orbit, propelled by the swollen cock outlined against her thigh.

*Hard, hard, hard to explain. Spit it out.* She drew a breath and forced herself to speak. "I think news will broadcast everywhere saying all the honeymoons were extended without charge while homes are being readied. Then some made up catastrophe happens within domes constructed as cheaply and fake as possible, to explain deaths which are actually murders —"

Her words froze as his hand pushed between her legs to cup her sex. Any cognitive ability she had went poof. She lurched into him, grinding down and — *goddamn bastard*—he withdrew his hand and stepped back. Her throat closed up. She couldn't speak if her life depended on it. Well, it probably did, and clearly he didn't believe… What was he doing?

He unzipped, leaving his pants low on his hips. Her heartbeat stuttered as he closed the gap between them, and a huge package humped into her stomach. "Your turn to trust," he muttered. "Name isn't Cooper, but Dexter, and not another soul knows what I plan. Has to stay that way. Gonna expose…more than myself. Don't involve yourself further or say a word to anyone. After I pretend to fuck you, link your wrist phone to mine, then walk out of here and stay low. Got it?"

*Oh my God, Sam Dexter? Oh no, no. This—his interest in the LC—is my fault?* Surprise crashed through her, almost making her forget the tension and ache, the need for his hand back where it'd been.

Samuel Dexter was the man behind *In the Loop*, one of the top political blogs in the world—a blog she'd commented on a month ago, wondering why someone didn't look into the suspicious soaring of the Love Center stock prices—as if a handful of the ultra-rich had reinforced a monopoly before the LC's launch of the much anticipated Lovers & Spouses in Space program. She'd remarked on the need for amateur sleuthing, then proceeded to do so herself. But so had he, damn him, obviously without asking for advice or help based on what he'd said—that no one else knew about his involvement with some plan or conspiracy.

She swallowed hard. *Holy crap. Sam Dexter.* Highly intelligent, but overly confident with a savior complex. A lone civilian shouldering this? He'd most likely get himself crucified, no matter how powerful his following was. She blurted, "That's bad…um…you bad naughty boy. I can help—oh!" *Hurt.* He'd spanked her.

He pulled his hand back, prepared to smack her on the butt again. "Remember the rules," he mumbled. "No screaming." He rubbed her backside, easing the sting. "How many guys have you toyed this long with? None like me, I expect, and it's time you stop playing risky games, little working girl." He jerked his head down to whisper, "I'm sorry. I didn't mean to hit you, but no—absolutely no. Too dangerous for you."

Pressure increasing, his hand forcibly eased apart her butt cheeks, and she couldn't help the fear shuddering through her.

He noticed. Smoothed his hand up for her waist and, to her astonishment, she wanted those fingers right back where they'd been. His touch—*honestly, Sam Dexter?*—stimulated her like no other, effectively erasing the memory of mere hours ago and another man mauling her backside.

*Get your signals right, idiot. This is your heart talking, as well as your libido. Forget the past before you lose the chance for a memory of a lifetime.*

She laid her palm on his arm, pushing down. His breath hitched as her chest molded into his. He shifted back, hand dipped back to cup her butt as his other wrapped around to fondle the edge of her breast through the thin cotton of her blouse.

"Shh, just tell me," he muttered. He rubbed against her, stroking and leaving her floundering as she tried to remember what he'd asked. How'd he expect her to understand coded script when he ignited every erogenous zone? *Think, Jenna. Think.*

He'd asked how many she'd managed to warn. He'd know the LC posted names of winners for the world to see.

She squirmed, his fingers beneath her skirt caressing against the sheer silk of her panties, and she fought to steady her voice. "I tried with four others. Three never showed and the one that did…went badly. You're the first to actually listen. I'll come—"

He nipped her ear. "There'll be no coming except… Sorry—on the edge here." He proved his point by homing in with his other hand, pressing panties and fingertips into her butt crack, leaving the rest of her screaming for attention. "I don't think I can stop the come about to happen, but the other will never happen. Understand?"

*Hell yes.* And she'd be damned if this gorgeous fool got off anywhere without some sort of backup. She could play dirty, as well.

*I want him. Honest to God, Sam Dexter in real time and space, in front of me.* He groaned as she grasped his waistband and shot her hand into his boxers.

A lovely dick leaped out to shake her hand, flesh against flesh, pre-cum oozing, and he growled. "Still can't—"

She squeezed.

He grunted. "Easy, you little witch."

"Difficult, you big…" *What the hell's the opposite of a witch? Who cares?* Rather beyond her to think past the word big. *Then stop thinking.* She drew her fingers up, caressing the delicious slope.

"You aren't"—his breath hitched as she stroked down—"listening."

"I am. And I insist on a finale I'm part of." His juicy cock pulsated in her grip, inch after inch after inch, all promising the ride of her life.

"Don't be an idiot," he snapped. "You have a death wish? Shouldn't I do all I can to end this without…er…pounding you so hard you can't move for two days?"

Two days until shuttles launched. She maintained her grasp on his cock. "Whatever. The price includes your happiness, not mine. In this moment, as well as what's ahead. Not as if your fiancée knows what you really desire, right? Is she as good as me, as understanding of how large *this* is?" She fondled him, tickling the pads of her fingers along the veins of his cock as her heartbeat jackhammered into her ribs. *Large, indeed. Oh my yes, he's perfect.* All she'd imagined and more. She couldn't let Sam Dexter stop *this* wondrous moment throbbing in her hand right now, then take *that* deadly ride without her.

"My intended is clueless," he grunted, hips bucking and cock shifting against her hold. "But remember, I didn't pay for *this*. I'm a loner who tries so hard to avoid harm to naïve brides. Call girls, that's different, yet the ending—no future—is not."

"Alone isn't good either. Gonna go splat, make a mess, without professional help." She dragged her hand north, reached his slippery crest, and slid her fingers south, increasing the tension winding within her to almost unbearable strain. "The clock's ticking, Mr. John. You afraid to lose control?"

He groaned and ran his hand up her thigh, curving back into her panties to head directly to Go. Rubbing lightly then harder, he circled and tap danced at her entrance. "Women, including you, are too hot to risk...I mean resist, but I'm taking a vow in two days. Like I said—no future." Two of his fingers shot into her, plundering the wetness. "Oh God, you're tight." He held her weight as her knees buckled. His thumb rubbed and teased her clit. He lowered his head, groaning in her ear. "You gotta say no. Now."

"Yes," she croaked. She milked her hand along his length, teasing over the head, feeling the thin slit with the pad of her thumb.

His breath hissed between clenched teeth. "You want *this* for real?"

"I said yes." The words leaped out of her mouth.

"Promise. You're not to interfere with my life. Say yes again."

"Yes."

"Really?"

She released him, drew her hand out of his pants and flung her arm around his neck. "Please."

With a sharp snap of his wrist, her panties came down. He stumbled until his shoulders hit the door. He seized her hips, lifted her off her feet and she bent her knees forward. The powerful head of his cock hit the mark, found her more than ready, and she moaned as he filled her in a long, wonderful thrust.

She arched, he bucked and worked her back and forth, pulling out, pounding back in so deep and far she couldn't tell where he ended. Heat rushed up her spine, roared into her head and within an animalistic rutting of who knew how long except it wasn't long enough, she gasped her release into his chest and he did the same. Spurt after spurt, she never wanted it to end.

His murmur into her ear—"I'm sorry, sorry"— eventually penetrated the blissful spiral.

He eased her off his waist onto legs of satiated jelly and held her.

A kiss, butterfly sweet, on her forehead grounded her back into the reality of a restroom stall. She blinked open her eyes. The worry in his gaze was the catalyst for the best moment of her life to dissipate. She shifted back, taking her weight from him.

He shoved and pushed until his still-turgid cock disappeared as she yanked up panties and smoothed down her skirt.

"Thank you," he said in a flat voice. "You're well worth the extra."

She stiffened. Nothing but a business transaction to provide cover for her warning of a conspiracy he already knew about? That's all the five minutes of mind-blowing sex had been to him? "Extra?"

He stared at her, deep emerald eyes so dark he drew the soul right out of her. "A tip for services rendered to my satisfaction."

Oh right. He'd said he'd pay more if she whispered. The ruse so they could talk during this recorded show without triggering a signal boost so every word was caught on tape. She held out her arm and he pressed his wrist phone against hers.

His brow furrowed. "Never contact me again." He bent, kissed her cheek and murmured, "Stay out of bars and far away from me." Hand trembling, he opened the stall and gestured her ahead.

Without looking at him, her phone or the amount he'd given her, she forced herself forward.

*Holy hell, I don't even know her name.*

Sam did know the name of the woman sitting at the bar and staring daggers at the sweetest thing he'd ever had, in the briefest sexual encounter of his life, as she hurried for the exit.

*Crap. Busted.* And doomed to losing his cover as a newlywed. Goddamn, his luck sucked. For the first time since he'd chatted Laree up on that dating site, the woman had to be early, instead of her usual twenty minutes to an hour late.

"You fucker," Laree howled at him when he'd slunk close enough. She glanced at her wrist phone, and her gaze spit fire. "You emptied your account. One hundred thousand, six hundred and ninety-seven dollars and forty-eight cents for a two-dollar whore? In a filthy bar?"

*Christ – really?* More pissed over money than another woman. At least she hadn't figured out his real name, seen his actual worth. He still had plenty left for his parents to pay for his funeral or legal expenses, and, hopefully, the brave soul whose scent was on his fingers would use the economic boost to get safely clear of any ties to him – a terrorist – once things went south. Without a bride, chances of this nightmare going any other direction were nil.

Then why did the happy grin, the smug expression of a guy with a purring dick, fight to break out on his face?

A direct look at the woman he'd callously used worked to wilt him – not surprising, but still it rankled there wasn't a single tear, no hurt and confusion, nothing but anger on her face. At least there'd be no broken hearts for either, and perhaps, just maybe, not walking up that ramp on his arm meant she'd live to reel in someone else.

Laree's forehead pinched, lips pressed thin, before she opened her mouth. "I'm guessing you just paid an escort who was contracted and already compensated by some asshole friend of yours? Using a lawyer-free transaction that's irreversible without the agreement of the receiver. Are you insane? You're really broke? No hidden accounts?"

"Penniless. I also quit my job," he lied. She'd believed him to be a respectable stockbroker.

Expression stunned, she drew back as if he'd punched her.

*Figuratively, I, the biggest of bastards, did.* Popped her bubble to getting her dreams of that free castle in the sky.

"You think I'll finance our wedding and support some loser?" she snapped.

*No. I expect you to tell me to fuck off.* He grasped her shoulders. "I'm sorry. Very sorry. I'm a sick perv you'll never see again." *Except on the news.* He leaned and pecked a kiss on her cheek and released her. "Deny knowing anything."

She yanked off the ring, and slammed it down on the bar. "I don't understand. You said you loved me."

Barely tolerate, let alone love, but at least she'd live to dance on his grave. He'd leave her the ring to hock—her fingers already easing closer to reclaim it—and the stocks and bonds she'd find in his briefcase. Least he could do. Her other hand rose as high as her voice had been and she slapped his face. He absorbed the blow he deserved, pivoted on his heel and it was his turn to run.

Outside, no sexy and mysterious woman in sight, he headed for his secret lair. Unfortunately, without a bride on his arm, he'd have to move forward with plan B.

Purchasing an illegal handgun wasn't easy. Not since billions of all makes and models had been melted down, destroyed after the global ban went into effect. Only government agents, police and those who sat in mass transport driver seats—including cockpits—were licensed to carry anything other than stun guns, mace or compound bows during specific times of the year and with a hunting license to support it.

It'd be much easier to steal a legitimate gun. He'd have to put a serious dent into his flush bank account in order to get the address of the pilot on the shuttle roster for this city. Then he'd have to cross so many lines, commit acts he'd never imagined doing. Sweat broke out of every pore just thinking about it.

He walked blindly, his head spinning as the mental list of felonies grew. Lurk in the shadows, attack and kidnap, steal an identity and stash the guy somewhere, doctor that identity, and — *bloody balls* — ready to be a shy bloke who'd never faced any screen other than computer monitors in solitude and without video feed to anyone but his family, to play an Oscar-winning role.

*Fun times.* He squared his shoulders and strode faster.

# Chapter Four

Jenna picked up her pace. The automated trains that left every quarter-hour were deadly to attempt boarding if you didn't heed the large digital display — blood-red numbers showing the countdown to one tenth of a second until departure.

In a heavily populated city of drones who measured their lives in fraction of a second intervals instead of coffee spoons, no one cared how easy it'd be to have weight sensors hold the door until a person cleared the entrance or exit. At least once a month, some unfortunate lost inches off their backside, or worse, a foot, when they didn't clear the pane of unstoppable glass and steel doors zapping along its track to close, despite more than air and insects in the way.

She caught the northbound train with eleven-and-a-half seconds to spare. Once inside, Jenna stumbled against the console and lowered her wrist phone to scan payment. Heavy footsteps behind her told her some fool boarded on her heels. The click of glass locking in place, and a lack of screaming meant they'd made it intact.

Her side ached, breath hitching, as she headed down the aisle on the crowded train to collapse in the first open seat. Her leg against a large grocery bag, she submissively didn't try to claim a section of the armrest with the elderly woman taking up more than her share of space. For once, she didn't mind the close proximity to teeming numbers of humans. A protective bubble of happiness enclosed her as the reality of what'd happened sank in.

*I, no dream, had Sam Dexter's dick inside me.*

Since she was a child, she'd gobbled up political and social musings to try to decipher what was truth or fiction concerning the world she lived in. A decade ago, she'd been of age to join the working class after school. Then she had to limit her obsession with news to stolen moments when the cams weren't centered on her cubicle. She stopped randomly reading to concentrate on sites that most caught her attention, one of which was a guy not much older than her who steadily became more and more famous.

Weekly, she devoured Dexter's blog — *In the Loop* — as soon as possible after her wrist phone chimed to tell her he'd posted. His profile pic hadn't been updated in years, not since he'd written a controversial post about female versus male stalkers. Since then, he'd successfully dodged photographers attempting to show more than his written word on the Net. But she felt like the moment she'd seen him sitting at the bar, the name Sam should have rung bells and she should have known.

Throughout the years, a particular way he'd phrased something looped, as the blog name promised, over and over in her thoughts. Occasionally she'd find her hands wandering as she pretended he lay beside her in the darkness of her bedroom. Oh God, imagine if they had been on a comfortable bed surrounded by jasmine and candlelight, instead of florescent lights and shiny porcelain.

She shifted her hips in the hard seat, the pleasant sensation between her legs complaining that fast and furious had been wonderful, but over way too soon. Yet no matter the speed, she wished she could repeat the event every day and night and afternoon and times in between for the rest of her life.

*Yeah. Like that'd ever happen.* Thousands of women — and men — would kill to be with a renowned intellect that hid from the public eye in person, but bared his soul online with cryptic honesty. *In the Loop* had a fan base of millions.

For the past three years, Dexter had been included in *Timeless Mag's* annual shortlist of most desirable bachelors, despite the lack of picture beside his attributes. Shortly after he first made the cut and successfully petitioned the magazine to skip even old photos, he'd blogged about attraction for reasons other than outer beauty. Said he wasn't a mysterious *Phantom of the Opera* guy, but he didn't need the acclaim. Preferred to remain anonymous to better maintain the integrity of his blog instead of the other option, becoming a recluse while his face flashed across screens and hiring bodyguards to protect from overly affectionate followers and paparazzi who learned his identity.

Jenna couldn't help wondering how many affectionate followers he didn't hide from. She raised her hand to her nose. The tangy male scent faded, and she clenched her fingers into a fist. *I held his dick.* But she hadn't traced her fingers over his face — features that promised to be plastered over the Net two days from now, regardless of what condition he was in.

Her throat clogged as her thoughts turned dark. Perhaps it'd be more than his face the world would see—a full show of that long lean body, a bullet-riddled corpse en route to cremation. More likely, he'd disappear never to be heard from, let alone seen, again.

She swallowed hard. After giving her the climax of a lifetime, Sam would have dealt with the model-perfect woman who'd stared death rays at Jenna leaving the bar. He'd have then followed in her tracks, but instead of hopping a train to obscurity, he would jump aboard the Stubborn Bastard Express, determined to expose a possible conspiracy without risking anyone but himself.

Over her dead body—and—*shudder*—that could literally come to be.

Did all his lovers have movie star looks like the one she presumed was his fiancée? Was the stunning blonde perched on the barstool more than a prop, someone he sincerely wanted to share vows with? The pair was gorgeous enough to get every perk a shallow world had to offer. No petition of theirs to be fruitful and multiply would be turned down.

Her spine stiffened. The next thought racing through her mind—*we didn't use protection*—grabbed her by the throat and shook her so hard her heart smacked into her ribs.

Billions of sperm—zillions, based on how powerfully he'd pumped—swam within her, each carrying the code of the man that he was—a man she'd admired for years, since she'd become his twenty-first follower on his third blog post.

Finding herself knocked up by a guy she had an intellectual thing for—and now a physical one—would be brilliant if she wasn't a fool and a liar. She'd told him she was sterile. Her teeth clenched, jaw aching as she gave herself a mental slap upside the head.

She gleaned by reading stories concerning working guys and gals, that a big draw for escorts over unpaid buddies was the male could go bareback. Anyone who practiced the world's oldest profession who wasn't sterile and documented on a regular basis as disease-free faced incarceration for twenty-to-life, or worse—being tossed in a trunk and driven to a shallow grave.

The woman beside her flashed a worried look and Jenna forcibly relaxed. *Crap* and *oh God* and *how-stupid-can-a-girl-get* turned into *why care*. Sam Dexter had told her to never contact him again. His welfare versus that of a possible child was a no-brainer. Any spark of self-preservation—doubt if she should do as he said and not risk herself—disappeared.

She'd sacrifice everything for her lover of five minutes, meaning a potential embryo of about eight cells after two or three days of life wouldn't grow any further, not with a mother refusing to let a man whom the world needed stop her from taking the crime of terrorist onto her own shoulders.

Unlike some sort of martyr-type plan Sam must have, odds were strong she'd survive whatever scheme she'd manage in the next forty-eight hours. She also knew she could at least put a crack in the powerful façade of the Love Center, encourage the smarter honeymooners to get the potential of a deadly hoax and thus save a few lives while sacrificing any possibility of offspring of her own. She'd be arrested, interrogated, beaten, cleaned up and sterilized, then locked away for life.

Her head hummed as the city flew by and she sat and pondered—for the umpteenth time—why she valued life so little. There'd been no motive for her to play with fire and invite strangers to bars, other than a sense of civic duty. A fool with an overdeveloped conscience. An inability to ignore — or better yet smush — the Jiminy Cricket lecturing in her ear, insisting Miss Pinocchio should do anything and everything in an uncaring world to step up and protect her fellow humans.

She'd planned to recruit a honeymoon winner, get him to check out her unsubstantiated suspicions, be alert to anything amiss when he boarded the shuttle with his bride. Not in her wildest dreams had she expected not only would that honeymoon winner be an idol of hers, but the fact Sam was suspicious of the LC as well added a huge wallop of credibility to her fears.

Seeing as it was quite possible she'd been the anonymous commentator to spur him into this particular line of investigative journalism, certain to have come to the same conclusions as her — the main one being that for some reason the LC had a problem with sterilized and gay couples — rushes of guilt scrambled up and down her spine.

Her leg maintained a steady jitter as her agitation grew stronger. There was much to accomplish before the shuttles ignited. The screen dominating each glass wall of the train showed her apartment building was in three stops. A hard jog would calm her, making her more productive. The life of a good man depended on her doing more than pining for his child or his love, which she never really had to begin with.

She stood and moved briskly down the aisle for the queue forming by the closest exit. No concern for the handicapped on the Metrarail, only the nimble dared board. If the line was too long and the door closed in her face, she'd be positioned to hop from the bullet train at the next stop.

Only ten people ahead, she disembarked with eight seconds of grace. Once again someone was behind her, but if she turned to look, she'd delay getting a handle on what had to be a perfected agenda. She needed a plan—a foolproof one—and so far she'd done nothing except bounce between depression and feeling like bursting into the *Zip-a-Dee-Doo-Dah* song. *Sam Dexter held me, kissed me, fucked…made love to me. Me, Jenna Jensen.*

She pounded the pavement at a steady pace, oblivious to her surroundings as deep green eyes danced in her head and wheels turned. When the skyscraper she called home loomed, she slowed and wiped the sweat from her brow.

She headed round back to the less trafficked entrance and stairs spiraling up and up, apartments getting cheaper the farther into the clouds one lived. Barely breathing hard, she'd jog up the steps in sync with the beat of an idea percolating in her brain.

Except—*tempest fugit.* Better take the elevator. Skip the shower. Keep the feel and scent of her lover close for a few hours at least. She carried a spark of desperate hope that maybe, just maybe, what happened had been something a bit more than an act taken too far for him — that at least affection at first sight, first touch, first kiss was actually possible. He'd held her as if he treasured her. Looked so sad after he'd kissed her goodbye on the forehead. As for herself, she'd loved him since she'd read his first blog post.

She felt her cheeks sizzle as a major plus to interfering with Sam occurred to her. She'd get a glimpse of more than a hot frontside. She'd have backside mental images as well to dwell on while doing laundry or peeling potatoes, hoarding bars of soap, staring at the gray walls of a cell. Of course not much, no bottom, she snickered to herself, could top the sight of his cock grasped in her hand, as long as she got over the fact she'd not had the chance to taste as well. She smiled as she thrust her wrist phone at the building's door to unlock it. *I'll save his fine butt, whether he likes it or not.*

A few steps into the dark corridor and the foot coming down behind her, catching the door, froze her limbs.

"Hey, wait up. I think I recognize that ass, but let me be sure."

The guy's voice sounded frighteningly familiar. She twirled to face — Gary Fenton?

Fenton gave a clipped nod, his way of saying they knew each other.

Fear twisted her gut, and her lungs locked as she took in the closed exit he blocked. Her gaze darted from his smirk to acknowledge the deserted corridor.

"I'm so glad you remember me," he whispered.

Right. Like she'd forget two days ago, the worst afternoon of her life. Another winner with the Love Center, Fenton was scheduled to depart on the same shuttle as Sam. She'd had Fenton's arms around her in the same bathroom. Unlike Sam, he'd unzipped before he'd opened the stall door. She'd barely had a second to grab the pill from her pocket and throw it in her mouth. His pale blue eyes lit with heat like they were now. Fenton had grabbed her, spun her, clamped his hand over her mouth then wedged his knee between her legs.

She hadn't been able to speak a word, let alone get him on board with honeymoons from hell. Her struggling, jerking as if she was having convulsions, didn't deter him from shoving his hand and her face to the wall and gleefully muttering in her ear.

*"Hell yes. Except I bet any friend of my brother's didn't pay for long. A looker like you must be a fortune. I also can't believe he even has a friend who thinks that schmuck could*

*get it up for more than a lap dance.*" He'd ripped one-handed at her slacks, popping the button, yanking them down with panties. "*I better take your ass first, in case there's a pimp busting in here soon. Hope you're not ready. The tighter the better.*"

She'd chomped at the pill, catching the inside of her cheek, stopped breathing and went limp.

"*Damn it. You want to do this on the floor? Stand up, loosen up, before I tear you up.*" He'd arched, jabbed at her, drawn back, readying to jackhammer — and, thank God, stopped.

Drops of her blood mixed in with induced spittle had splattered between his fingers gripping her mouth, over his arm, and the fact she didn't respond to his cock, mercifully small, did the trick. At the time, the irony of her thoughts about doing or not doing the trick helped her pretend she was in the midst of a nightmare she'd soon wake from.

He'd gasped and dropped her — stared down at her collapsed body, her gaze deliberately fixed, bloody froth bubbling from her slack mouth, then ran. Ten minutes later she'd stopped heaving into the sink, cleaned herself up and left, wishing Gary Fenton would get close and personal with the front grill of an obsolete bus like the handicapped and elderly used before he dragged some dewy-eyed bride onto a lunar shuttle.

And here she was, facing the same guy again who reeked with anticipation and righteous strength. The floor was eerily quiet. People were at work or locked safely in their soundproof homes. Looked like she wasn't about to get her wish that Fenton would drop dead. Karma stabbing her where it hurt because she'd prayed for worms to eat out his heart?

*Run, idiot, run.* She tensed, but he was already coiled. A cobra about to strike, he was too close. She'd not make it far.

That large hand shot out. He grasped her arm and she swallowed her scream. "It took me a while to get it," he said. "Some sort of pill to fake all that crap coming from your mouth." He shook her hard enough to rattle her teeth. "The scam being I'd not say a word about a dead hooker and you'd get paid for nothing."

All she'd wanted to do was find someone already on the shuttle's manifest who'd board and look for evidence that she was or wasn't delusional, get authorities and press involved as needed. Flood the Net with pics before they landed on the moon to find nothing behind the curtain of a paradise getaway except crematoriums.

In retrospect, it was a half-assed plan doomed to go wrong. She could have done something less altruistic but so much safer, such as screw with a guy's heart. Have sex, pretend to care in the off chance he'd fall for her and propose.

Most of all, armed with nothing but pills then pepper spray, she shouldn't have dealt with strangers. A smart woman would have involved a cop who'd stick his neck out with her, play the part of a groom and not just cuff her and cart her off to a psych ward. All she had to do was tell the truth. Risk some randomly picked officer would not only believe her, but that he was neither on the payroll of the LC nor would he unwittingly alert any authorities that were, leaving them to disappear the problem by a bullet in her forehead as well as his.

Instead, she'd stuck with the idea of recruiting a groom. Never expecting there'd be any way the second guy would have a sort of connection to her, and the first would be so into entitlement he'd stop at nothing to get satisfaction.

Oh God. After spending ridiculous amounts on illegal wrist phones, she sincerely wished she'd picked Sam before she'd contacted Fenton.

Fenton must have gone back to the bar, waiting for God knows how long, hoping she'd return, which was exactly what she'd done. Like an idiot, she'd texted Sam to meet her at the same bar — the cleanest one she could find with a large bathroom that had an inside lock on the door.

She fought to keep her face blank. "Let go. Please. You don't understand. No one hired me. I was trying to warn you about the Love Center. Your life is in danger. If you get married and board that shuttle, you'll probably die."

Fenton burst out laughing. "You found me on the winner list. Next you'll tell me you'll have a chat with my bride unless I pay a fortune." He began dragging her toward the stairs. "Which floor is yours, whore? I won't wait long. No worries. The stairwell will do to start."

She dug her heels in and he stopped.

"The angrier I am," he snapped, "the more I'll —"

She clawed out, raking his skin under her fingertips.

He jerked loose and chuckled. "That's all you have? You fight like a girl. Hey, if I was a shmuck who'd pay, how much does it cost for upscale pussy like yours?"

She reached for her wrist phone. Thank God for the scientist — a woman — who'd perfected the ability to electronically transmit DNA directly to local authorities.

Fenton grabbed her elbow, squeezed and released her. He thrust his face inches from hers and winked. "Go ahead. Press the rape-in-progress app. I'll pop up as a sterilized male who hasn't left a bruise—yet." His grin widened as he straightened. "Police will rush here within hours. After they take care of all the fertile males getting what was promised them."

A sob welled in her throat. Sam had recently done a blog post claiming that very thing. He'd come up with stats that one out of a hundred women, and one out of forty girls or boys would be raped at least once in their lifetime, with males who were sterilized getting but a high-five slap of one to ten years, based on whether or not loved ones of the victim raised a public outcry.

Non-neutered rapists were guaranteed twenty years to life, depending on severity and whether a survivor finding herself pregnant didn't willingly run to get an abortion. Standard admitting procedure for prisons in every nation included delousing, shaving and sterilization before handing the convict an orange jumpsuit.

Fenton's claim to being infertile didn't make sense. "Then…how did you win a honeymoon?"

He scowled. "I applied, you little fool. How else?"

She swallowed hard. Might as well keep him talking. Maybe someone would come. "I…um…had access to databases. A friend of a friend works at one of the LC hubs. She said as far as she could tell, only the applicants whose background showed no record of being incarcerated or voluntarily sterilized were chosen."

Fenton threw his head back and snickered. "Ahh. Caught me. I didn't actually win. My twin brother filed and paid for the marriage license. I made sure he thought he stayed the loser that he is and seduced his slob of a fiancée. A few pics of my brother with his hands all over a male hooker had her blubbering on my shoulder. Then I showed her some real dick. She agreed she'd be my bride and switched his and my wrist phones. What better way to leave my brother to deal with scumball collectors than disappearing off the face of the Earth... Why am I telling you this?"

*Christ, really? He's this much of an asshole?* She stiffened. "Why indeed? You'll screw over your brother, renege on gangsters, loan sharks or whatever but you hung out for hours then stalked me because you think I was paid for sex you didn't get?"

He jerked her forward, his hold on her arm so tight she could feel the bruise forming. "That's right, sister. But I'm a nice guy. You can suck your way into my good graces. Then decide if it's face against the wall or the steps." He released her, undid his buckle and started to unzip. "You owe me, so stop whining."

Whining? Jesus. She didn't have time for this creep, for a rape on a stairwell or anywhere. Victims — the underdogs — needed the voice of people like Sam Dexter. To implement some sort of plan to help him, she had to burn through multiple firewalls and hire felons who may or may not have the ability to burrow into impenetrable security files. She needed documented proof showing the intense propaganda — contests to win free homes that flooded every advertising spot on the Net for months — wasn't just aimed at recruiting couples to jump into marriage with the only benefit to the LC being a thousand dollar a pop licensing fee. Concrete evidence exposing a hidden agenda, other than wanting to ease the stressed resources of Earth by spending billions to make dreams come true, had to be out there.

So, she had to come up with more funds and a higher credit limit than her bank account held, as well as time and time and more time to forge credentials, change names and so on, while begging everyone she knew to loan her every cent they had so she could hire cyber-tech experts who wouldn't take an IOU for payment.

She stopped chewing the inside of her cheek and braced to do whatever she had to in order to free herself from the two hundred plus pound obstacle presently in her way.

"Fine. I'll make things right." She forced a smile and averted her gaze from his open pants. "No need to get nasty or to risk someone finding us." She gestured forward. "Apartment 102 is vacant. I...er...have an arrangement with the landlord. No alarms when I unlock the door. I swear."

Fenton licked his lips and glanced down the hall ten feet to number 102.

The moment his head turned, she grabbed the pepper spray out of her pocket, raised her arm, shot him directly in the eyes and ran.

His screams rang in her ears as she flung herself out of the building into the street.

She heard him again, his bellow now filled with rage, as she raced around the corner into an area of bustling commerce. A desperate burst of speed shot her toward a café. She bounded through the opening door and came to a grinding halt. The clawing stitch in her side threatened to drop her to the floor of the crowded coffee shop. Jenna sucked in a deep lungful as she raised her head.

Thank all and any deity who watched over fools that there were no monsters in sight, just strong-looking men and women smiling and chatting in every corner. A shiver went through her, nerves raw and skin itching, and she swallowed hard. She'd curl into a whimpering ball later. Difficult as it was, despite the horror churning within over what had almost happened, she—girl with agenda—needed to snap herself together.

The woman wearing a bright pink hat who'd held the door tsked. "Caffeine is a powerful addiction, young lady. Is it really that bad?"

She forced a smile. "It is. Um...maybe I could buy you a cup? I'd love to talk to someone." *And borrow your wrist phone to access the Net after pretending mine's broken.*

If there wasn't an 'arrest and interrogate' flag beside her name yet, there would be after she clicked on links to the latest terrorist sites, connections with the means and know-how to guide her toward purchasing what she'd need to get on that shuttle. The Net was free worldwide, but there wasn't a single web strand of cyberspace that Big Brother didn't have eyes on.

The woman returned her smile and nodded. Jenna headed for the automated machine while her new friend grabbed a table.

Twenty frickin' dollars for two small coffees? Guess she hadn't been in a café in a while. She sighed, glancing at her wrist phone as she scanned payment. Her jaw dropped. *Am I hallucinating? What the hell?* Way too many zeroes. She blinked hard, then again, but the number didn't change.

How? Banks never made mistakes—not in this day and age.

Occam's razor—the theory that the simplest answer was most often the correct one—still held true, and a jolt of warmth hit her. Sam had transferred over a hundred grand into her account. Most likely all he had. The sort of thing a kind but doomed man would do.

The heat within her birthed into a sizzling ball of starlight, crackling from head to toe.

She set one of the coffees down at the table of a shabbily dressed man, nodded and hurried on to join the woman with a pink hat. She'd tell her she'd seen the light regarding addictions, but hoped she could borrow her wrist phone to get online. Pretend that hers wasn't working.

After all, who needed a cup of Joe, or any other guy not named Sam, for that matter. Jenna had more than enough energy to fuel herself for forty-eight hours of relentless preparation then some.

# Chapter Five

In his cubbyhole of a single's apartment, Sam powered up the com-desk and wished he lived in a future where he could hit an app that'd function to hook a caffeine drip directly to his arm. So much to do, and he'd forgotten to grab a cup before coming home to a depressingly deleted lair. On the fifty-sixth floor, in the low-rent skyscraper on the outskirts of the metropolis he'd taken a suitcase to five weeks ago, and not a single bean of salvation from fatigue in the dump.

With a heavy sigh, he tapped in the complicated security code and opened a fresh page on his blog. The sun was going to rise in less than six hours, and launch day would begin. He had little time and much to do to implement Plan B.

The problem? His head whirled. Emotions in turmoil with the schoolboy funk of feeling as if an arrow had hit, smack dab into his chest. He'd perform better if he took a moment to yank out the stench of Cupid, allowing himself to concentrate on becoming a hardened criminal without distraction.

A search pulled up hundreds of images. He picked a pair of swans standing nose to nose, heads dipped with long necks forming the sappy image of a heart and feet posed on crisp snow beside a dappled lake. He loaded the image and began to type.

*Do I – a male in my prime with potentially thousands of lovers – have the* cajones *to admit I wish to evolve – to pattern my future like the lowly three-to-five percent of the animal gene pool? That the aftermath of a ten-minute encounter showed me the path of a monogamous Mexican gray wolf is my true desire? A French angelfish is another example, as is the black vulture. I'd not ever be shunned by my fellow bone-pickers because I'd never betray the partner who shares my nest.*

*History has shown few humans – and even fewer animals – have a mate-for-life mentality ingrained in their genetic code. As of three hours, twenty-two minutes ago, I can honestly say I no longer fantasize if there's anyone able to make me aspire to sign my name on that short list.*

*Love at first sight – is it possible?*

*I sit and reason and my heartbeat stutters – hell yes – and my dick squirms – not sure, but fuckin' why not? – while flashes of memory push my blood to return south. I grow harder and harder, and logic becomes more and more of a struggle as cock agrees with heart.*

*In the lesser times of yesterday, I was a simple, solid XY type who stood firmly disillusioned with sons, brothers, fathers and uncles everywhere. Not once in my enlightened past was I duped to believe that Santa Claus, a God born of a virgin, fresh maidens awaiting my virtual dick in a paradise or halls of Valhalla or any of the romantic notions sentimentalists have yammered about for eons were possible. I've belched and laughed in a reclining group of males, sports on the twenty foot ceiling and wall screens, and platters heaped with charred meat doused with globs of heart attack inducing – genetically modified to be a murder weapon – Red Savina habanero sauce. Fists at the ready to defend my right to scoff at the parade of commercials, I thought myself immune to things that lesser schmucks fall prey to, as portrayed in so many lovey-dovey ads on the sidelines of televised events.*

*Love at first sight? Nah. I'm not wrong in thinking that's bull. It took more than my eyes drawn to a curvaceous form I could lift and hug in one arm. It – that instantaneous and hopeful and wondrous attraction labeled love – required first whiff, first words, first touch, first kiss and first time with my back to a restroom wall and her legs clamped round my waist.*

*Ungodly provocative, she smelled of vanilla, strawberries and cream accented with specks of nutmeg. The color of tree bark, overturned sod, melted dark chocolate, her beautiful eyes spilled with emotion – doubt, lust and intelligence.*

*Her fear – downcast gaze, white knuckles, trembling lower lip, hand fumbling for a weapon – sliced through every defense I've built within thirty years of life as a guy destined to posture on the pinnacle of the food chain. Her worry made...*makes *me yearn to be a better man. I gave in to a worried urge to spank her. Not that hard, but the awareness I should do more, shake her and not stop until common sense reminded her she really should pepper spray the fuck out of a stranger with his back to the only exit, went poof as my cock grew achingly more insistent.*

*It should have required the stamina of an overused bull elephant, but it was damn easy to hold my growling dick in check because that fear, her uneasy acceptance I could do as I will, made the myth of love at first sight futile and potentially impotent if the attraction isn't – I mean* wasn't *– reciprocated.*

*If it – sex – was only an itch, a means to make a living or a way to deal with an aroused guy without getting bruised then flee to shower and forget, I wouldn't be pondering the validity of love sonnets in this moment.*

*In that moment – my hand close yet not plundering, my cock swollen and drooling but confined – I waited. Kept the brutish impulse to strip clothing and feast with love at first sight upon every exposed inch of her reined in, until she took the lead.*

*Once she did, it was too late to care about clothing in the way. I can still feel in my bones – my favorite one throbbing anxiously as I sit here and remember her confident grasp and stroke of my cock as she freed me from my boxers. Joy, joy, joy was mine when her fingers told me she was in as deep lust as I.*

*The glue that took the encounter past impulsive male-female chemistry, beyond a fast and furiously hot fuck, was when I jerked my gaze from her hand teasing my thrilled cock to see the intelligence sparkle from those sweet brown eyes. That spark within her expression – confirmation she knew what she wanted and that it was me – rocked me to the core, and she fucked my brain before she satisfied my dick. I was amazed to find myself humbled before I even penetrated her.*

*Love at first touch was a two-way street and I could tell the reason she'd been frightened, the purpose for the encounter no less, was no longer something she thought about as she gave consent. I felt the wetness in her panties, muscles quivering in her thighs making it clear when she said yes she offered much more than slam-bam-thank you-move on. Her caress of my cock promised every dream of true love an experienced man, suddenly rendered a schoolboy, could imagine.*

*I hitched her skirt up farther, tore off panties and held skin so soft and silky I worried I grasped her too tightly. My rough hands must have imprinted on, bitten into the deliciously rounded cheeks of her ass that fit so ably between my sweating palms. I drove in and out of moist, tight heaven, holding her weight with ease, and she mewled, made erotically soft gasping noises against my chest and into my mouth. Sweat dripped down my back, her wetness clung, squeezed and held to me as we took rutting to a level I'd never felt before.*

*I never wanted it to end.*

*Inevitable climax is a manic drive all life pulsates toward. Serotonins exploding and neurons rocketing with ecstasy as hormonal fluids and semen gush free is the end goal, yes.*

*But in that unique encounter, I spent myself in magical bursts of mental doors opening into the realm of actual soulmates. A red-blooded, thickheaded man is typing the following words with all earnestness. I ejaculated into not only her, but the land of happy-ever-after. The chemical draw, covalent bonds formed when I plunged in balls-kissing-ass deep, then those magnetically charged bonds bending as my cock withdrew against her clamping muscles, left me wishing I could freeze time. Hold to a fucking moment of spontaneous combustion, an impossible attraction of fitting together that I'd never achieved before.*

*I yearn to recapture that moment when two bodies became as close as they could possibly be without devouring the other. Before my erupting cock and her contracting warmth and spasms warned the cliché is true, that all good things must cum to the end.*

*And once the haze of satisfaction lifted, damnable reality intruded to rip apart bonded souls from both sides and within the rainbow. Grounded here on a lonely Earth, I must find her – have her again. See if it – she – is as real, life changing as I think she is.*

*Sweetheart – are you out there? Reading these words? I want you. Your lips on my mouth, my chest, my cock, my ass, then resting over my heart. I want to hold and have and have and have you safely in my arms for a lifetime. I want to cherish you. Until death…*

*Jesus, Dexter, snap out of this.* He jerked his hand up to slap himself upside the head and slumped. He was parted from the woman whose name he didn't know, and not by death or a prison cell — yet. There wasn't a damn thing a good man would do about it. His hands wilted over the com-desk as his dick followed suit to sob against his thigh.

What the fuck was he playing at? Christ almighty. His dick wept for a love at first plunge that had lasted all of ten frickin' minutes? He snorted and scrubbed his face, wiping away tension while his hand shot out to delete every maudlin word.

His stomach clenched as he erased all but the picture of the pair of swans. Beneath that, he slapped up a disclaimer saying sorry, but he was closed to comments until further notice. For the first — *fuck it, shut up* — time he logged out of his blog so he'd not even know how many readers attempted to comment.

He couldn't leave the woman clued in to this unsubstantiated conspiracy any means to persuade him he should risk her neck as well. Super-idiot had to fly solo. He glanced at the time — 12:05 a.m. — and damn soon. Activating every spyware safety protocol he knew, he began surfing.

Two fourteen a.m. and Sam closed out. He hadn't paused until he had what he needed, despite his growing thirst. He pushed to his feet, walked two feet and opened the mini-fridge. Bypassing the glittering bottle of Cristal, fresh in 2030 from the polluted vineyards of France, he grabbed the second most expensive item in the place — a quart bottle of Russian vodka.

Some things never seemed to change. Pockets of snotty Americans pretended as if borders to Mexico and Canada still existed, shoddy product from Asia filled discount stores worldwide and the priciest, most lethal alcohols came from the UKE, United Kingdoms of Eurasia.

Cool and sharp, the gulp of liquor slid down to hit his gut with a splash of acidic courage. He set the bottle on top of the mini-fridge and wiped his brow. His hands clammy, a shallow inhale filled his lungs with the stench of fear. The musk of a moose about to have a pack of wolves — mated pairs working side by side — launch into his hindquarters then his throat, settled about him.

He sighed. He had many regrets, and the most recent one was washing his face and hands before the numbing hours online. He raised his right hand beneath flared nostrils, drew a sharp breath and swallowed hard. Not a trace, a single sugar and spice whiff of the most beautiful woman, remained on the fingers he balled into a fist.

*Stop thinking about her, asshole.* He had to forget women, the woman, the one, love at first sight, taste, feel — tight and wet and perfect...*shut up.* He grasped the bottle and downed another swig. Time to concentrate on the guy — Roger Moore, who resided at 1515th St, 76-18 — he'd mentally drawn a red circle around, after scanning his wrist phone to take a large chunk out of his primary bank account.

It cost ten grand for the name and address. Twenty more purchased the informant's silence if that name happened to appear in the obituary column. It didn't seem right a man's life could be worth so little. He'd expected triple — thirty thou, at the very least.

Sam shook his head, tossed the vodka back in the fridge and grabbed the champagne. He'd intended it for Laree. Had plans of making sure she was pleasantly drunk so she'd sleep soundly on this night that should have been the last he shared her bed. Now it'd make a decent weapon to bash a guy over the head.

Once the deed was done, the licensed gun and wrist phone of a pilot in hand, should he destroy the computer here? Is that what an honest criminal did to protect the source? Most likely it'd be pointless. No matter how beaten and broken the computer, a good tech could salvage data unless Sam torched the com-desk using a highly combustible accelerant, and no way would he risk harm to the hundreds in this building who'd stampede for elevators and stairs when smoke alarms blared and sprinklers burst on.

His mouth gritty with alcohol, he spit into the bathroom sink and stalked to the single mattress pushed in the corner. He grabbed the duffel bag sitting on it and exited the apartment.

Two thirty-five a.m. on what should have been his last night with his fiancée as a single man, although a con artist. His brain hissed in protest, heartbeat slowed, dick shrank and toes curled inside his heavy boots. It seemed all parts of him agreed. He didn't ever want to see a blonde twirling in a white gown, diamond sparkling on her finger, yammering her friends will be so jealous, again. He'd rot in hell for using Laree so callously, but damn. If the woman hadn't been that self-absorbed, it stood to reason she'd have outed him for the manipulative prick he was.

On the ground floor, Sam pushed open the door and left the building. The full moon competed with compressed buildings to blot out the skyline glowing with neon lights. High in the sky, the lunar satellite cast silvery shadows and beckoned lovers to their fate.

The bullet train took him to 1000th street, and a somewhat crowded bus on a planet that never slept carried him deeper, past the heart of the city. Street lights became spaced farther and farther apart, and the scruffs of grass spiking up between cracks of concrete harder to see.

He darted his gaze, checking out but not lingering on the two dozen or so faces surrounding him. Only a few women were sitting close to their guy, no children, but any of these men on their way home after work or a night out celebrating could have a tiny black box tucked in their pocket. The man would either be gathering courage to propose, or he'd have said yes to the guy or girl who'd popped the question to him and had high hopes of getting in on next month's full moon action. He'd be preparing to ride a rocket to a happy life that, in a promised six months, would include functional and free Net to all the planets, including Earth. Then he could earn a living connected beyond the stars, his territory marked by that white picket fence round a five-bedroom abode and desert landscaped lawn on Mars.

Far, far away from that reality, on a lonely and overcrowded blue planet, no one returned Sam's furtive glances and he huddled into himself.

He got off five blocks before his destination and ran. The cool air felt wonderful on his face and he pushed himself, but as the address grew closer, he understood he could have skipped the exertion. No worries about someone eyeballing him, taking in his features and reporting his presence to authorities after his picture sprawled all over the Net. The few other joggers he passed kept their gaze averted. So much for Neighborhood Watches and concerned citizen laws.

He slowed and hunched his shoulders as he strode on the glittering sidewalk to the entrance. Beneath the bright moon, the trapped energy of the sun resonated in every laminated seam of inch-by-inch solargridding. He wished the energized walkways had the ability to do more than repel cold and snow and light. Sending a high voltage charge up his leg would help cattle-prod a progressive guy from devolving to a caveman.

*What other choice do I have?* He sighed. Time to psych himself up to bust open another stereotype — all men are capable of unjust violence — he hadn't thought pertained to him. If love at first sight was real, then certainly someone with his size and strength could easily beat another into submission if he got the jump on...him — a pilot about to be world-renowned? If the man wasn't already famous?

Oh God. He was a pathetic supervillain. He should have thought the breaking-entering-assaulting thing out thoroughly. The guy would be a handsome aerospace engineer chosen to pilot a frickin' shuttle to the moon, meaning he wouldn't be alone. He'd be in bed, getting the rest he needed to make history, come dawn. His glamorous wife would be using his perfect six-pack abs for a pillow, while the allotted child, a cooing baby girl, cuddled her teddy in a crib in the same room. Or a bachelor, the pilot would have twins either side as he sprawled in his satin-sheeted bed, custom-made to be the size of an apartment, a queue of beauties waiting in his luxurious suite that took up an entire floor.

But then why'd this hotshot pilot live in the crappy side of the city, in the seediest 'scraper that didn't have more than three security cams on the rear entrance? There wasn't a phone-swipe key box in sight to enter the building. Not even a lame-ass cheap one.

Sam mentally shrugged, ducked his head and yanked open the building's door to slither in. He stared at the dull red carpet and hurried for the elevator. Once inside, he ignored the cams above his head in each of four corners and tapped the dull gold 76.

The elevator, which reeked of what he feared was semen and piss, slowly worked its cables to go higher and higher. With an unpleasant lurch, it finally halted and the doors opened to an empty corridor.

He eased the duffel bag off his shoulder as he crept toward number eighteen and unzipped it. He stopped beside number seventeen. Stomach in knots, his presence being recorded on at least one cam, he yanked off his sweat-soaked shirt and pulled out what would have been the seamless, white uniform top of a delivery service employee if he hadn't wadded it up in the bag.

A moment later, the bag sat on the floor beside the door labeled eighteen, the bottle of Cristal was in his hand, and instead of throwing up, Sam pushed the buzzer.

Nothing.

He tapped the buzzer again. Waited five minutes and hit it once more, this time keeping his finger pressed down. The time clicked away on his wrist phone for another half a minute before the com opened.

"Whaaat?" The rough voice, thankfully male, sounded slurred and furious.

"Sir, I am so sorry. Please. I have a gift from the Love Center."

"The L…C? Why the fuck are you bringing it now?" The guy snorted. "Leave it by the door."

"I can't. It's too expensive. I was supposed to deliver hours ago, but I ran into some complications. Come sign for it and accept a Nixon from me for your trouble." The picture of the disgraced thirty-seventh president of the United States was on the two thousand dollar bill — a bit of a collector's item.

"Fuck. Hang on," the man muttered.

Sweat beaded on Sam's forehead, his hands shook and hard swallows kept the two gulps of vodka from coming back out.

The door flung open and the stench of cheap beer whacked him in the face. A ripped guy—wearing a spotted wife-beater style T-shirt and tighty-whities glared out of thin-slitted eyes. He raked his gaze from the bottle in Sam's hand, his other hand empty, to burn into his face.

"Two thousand, you said?" he snapped.

"Please keep your voice down so the cams don't trigger an alert. Are you Roger Moore? May I see some ID?"

"You can bite my ass, buddy. That Nixon?" the guy growled, but he'd kept his voice low.

"Er...I'll give you everything in my wallet—two of those bills—if you tell me if you're the pilot for the moon shuttle leaving in a few hours."

"Yes. Moore, that's me."

As if he'd trained for it all his life, Sam shoved his foot in the door and sucker punched the guy. The man grunted, fury filled his eyes, but he didn't get his arm out before the Cristal kissed him in the side of the skull and the big bad pilot went down.

The cam was recording away, but yippee, not a single yelp to trigger attention. Sam set the bottle inside and bent to hit the guy on the back of his head with his fist. The rough moan stopped. Moore collapsed and went still.

Took him a few seconds to yank Moore farther into the apartment and close the door. His heart in his throat, Sam felt for a pulse—strong and steady. His heart out of his throat and trying to strangle him with aortas clamped on either side of his neck, he let the guy down and hurried past the couch, floor littered with takeout and empty plastic bottles of beer, into the next room.

Relief hit him like a ton of lunar rock as he absorbed the fact there was no wife, husband, a child or even a playmate. The bed was messy and to his disgust, the black market and obsolete-in-this-era magazine had wadded tissues beside it, was open and exposing compromising pictures of a nude girl, eyes deadened, who couldn't have been more than fourteen.

He held back, but still allowed his boot to kick the unconscious pilot in the gut before he dragged him to the bedroom and hefted him onto the mattress.

His antique Boy Scout pocket knife, *Be Prepared* written in gold ink down the side, encouraged the sheet to tear easily. He bound Moore's hands and feet so tightly, he'd have welts. He made the gag loose enough the man could breathe, removed the wrist phone and pocketed it.

A thin, small, metal case lay on the floor in the corner and his trusty knife was useless. Damn thing wasn't at all prepared for the complexity of a measly lock. As expected, the blade broke as he tried to jimmy the carrier open. Sam shrugged and picked it up. He grabbed the uniform thrown over a chair, the cap on the floor beside it, and set the items down beside the door.

Outside, in front of the cam — *Christ, what's it matter at this point* — he retrieved the duffel bag then went back inside and tossed the delivery service jacket into the corner, a time bomb holding more of his DNA, but *c'est la vie*. He shoved the pilot's uniform and cap into the bag and grabbed the champagne and briefcase then exited. He waved the bottle at the cam as he slunk for the elevator.

The first person to make eye contact with him on the bus was an elderly man with a shrunken chest and work-worn hands clasped in his lap. At 1000th street, he silently handed the guy the champagne and hopped off.

Back at his apartment, Sam tossed the duffel bag on the table and set the metal case on the floor. He spread a towel on the four-by-four table, retrieved the pilot's uniform and laid the shirt out. A scan of his wrist phone over an app on the com-desk and a pre-heated ironing device popped up. He had ten minutes before it went cold and he'd have to pay another fifty dollars for five more minutes of heat.

He failed. Cost two hundred dollars before the jacket, shirt and pants were to his liking and hanging in the closet. That was the easy part.

Shaking exhaustion from his face, he headed out with the determination of a man about to cry wolf. He now had a less-shaky platform to stand on, thanks to the ominous metal case he'd found, as well as the guy who supposedly could fly a shuttle living in a seedy dump. It added up to justification he was onto something that'd definitely get him killed. Thank Christ he'd made sure the woman, whose hot and sweet and beautiful image had damn well better flash in front of his eyes before the bullets hit, was safely out of the game.

# Chapter Six

Jenna had tumbled not head but heart first into the game of whistleblower. Like playing Russian roulette with a full clip, the cost of failure was clear. Arranging for a misfire was the only chance. Without a single error, they had to get onboard, figure it out and alert the world as to what was happening before the LC pulled the trigger.

It'd been rather easy but quite costly to find someone with Net skills to far surpass hers. She now sat at her com-desk and hesitated, worried and facing the wide, green purchase button staring back at her.

Because of Sam, she had the funds to empty twenty thousand into this site that 'worked diligently to save whales from illegal poaching. These so-called environmentalists didn't offer specifics on how the rescue would happen within hours of receiving payment, nor did they claim satisfaction guaranteed.

There'd be no refund, and it was on her if she screwed-up when entering the encrypted coding to spell out what she really wanted. The info would be attached to the monies she sent, and her message—

hopefully after being read and understood by some criminal—would be irreversibly transposed into the name and stats on which whale owed a continued peaceful existence to her donation. Something she'd never have, not after she tapped that green button.

*Come on, get on with it.* It, the rescue, must be a hoax to cover up the illegal activity she really was paying for. Only the sickest of sociopaths hunted sea creatures with superior intellect and active social lives, most often even authorities didn't react if said hunter was found floating face down in the northern Pacific.

She'd read between the lines to understand her request to look for any unusual activity during the building of the shuttles—such as supplies purchased that didn't make sense for manned flights and to provide her with schematics of the pods that'd hold the honeymooners—would be processed by some genius who'd activate a program to overwrite her words so nothing remained visible to Big Brother other than the solicitation and her agreement to donate. *Just do it. Think green and move onward.*

She bit her lower lip, tapped the purchase button and sat back with Sam Dexter's deep green eyes on her mind. While she waited for the name of her whale, which she presumed would be long enough to print out in a page before the bulk of the info was deleted from the hard drive and cyberspace, the clock and her libido ticked onward.

*Hot, hard body.* Even if she managed to get an idea of what could go wrong once they were on the shuttle, she—overconfident fool that she was—had to get onto the damn thing first.

*Cocky smile.* It was stupid to put all the eggs, so to speak, into one basket by hoping these nature-loving rebels would figure that she also needed fake identification, meaning she had to make contact with yet another unsavory site. If only she, the clueless idiot going with instinct instead of logic, could make the right choice about whom to trust.

*Brilliant mind.* Her name and Sam's on that list as winners and the forged IDs imprinted into their wrist phones were next on her to-do list — and that had to cost more than twenty grand to accomplish.

*Strong, competent hands. Calloused finger pads of an expert writer and lover.* She flexed her dominant scrolling hand, danced her own worn fingers on the screen and was glad she'd already scrolled about yesterday, narrowing down options. She just had to make a few more decisions after getting an answer from her whale-loving friends. So, no reason to cease the distracting images of a certain good-looking guy that kept popping into her head, doing nothing other than making her moist between the legs. Why not play about the Net, encourage the touch of OCD within her concerning her rebellious streak when it came to Big Brother, as she waited?

The cobweb overlords, intricate spying sanctioned by governments worldwide, would mark the hops she made to red-flagged as well as frivolous sites. It was only a matter of time before authorities became clued into her cyber history. She may as well flitter about, check out what happy lovers were doing before potentially deadly shuttles fired up. Anything to make things slightly more confusing for the controlling bullies policing the Net.

She sucked at lying in both the cyber and real world. Minus any combat skills, knowing pepper spray wouldn't cut it, all she had was her intellect. And here she was, smiling at pics on Face2Face — the world's largest social site. Reading comments on whether the pink or purple spacesuit looked better with readily available steel-toed boots, or best go with the coveted, outrageously priced space boots that transformed into sleek and sexy heels.

Hopes, dreams, expectations concerning romance and happy-ever-afters posted and chirped from every locale on Earth. Grooms boasted of the novel or clichéd way they'd proposed. Bubbly brides postured, showing off outfits. Thousands of families celebrated and said their online goodbyes to the happy couples.

*What should I, the phony bride, wear?* On some shuttles, monochrome attire — traditional frilly white gowns and crisp white or black tuxedos — would fill the aisles. Red silk with intricate gold patterning would dominate other aircrafts.

*Hair up or down?* Women preened in their bright sarees, men in their japas or suits and many of both genders were draped in gold bling.

*Red or blush lipstick?* Brides displayed temporary henna tattoos, cheerfully and intricately painted, on hands and feet with an excess of color and an emphasis on shades of yellow to ward off evil and green for luck.

*God, I'm an idiot.* Luck and evil influenced by color choice wouldn't matter if she didn't figure out a way to get on that shuttle in any sort of get-up, then off without being in a body bag. A ping of an incoming message had her closing out windows and buckling down.

The message said her whale — Assion — was indeed in trouble and, *no duh*, time was critical. Her criminals were in the process of acquiring a local to provide her with the specialized medicine the young male needed to continue surviving in polluted waters. She should enlist, on her own, an alias such as Captain Ahab to find Moby D so he could be treated. If she did so, she could link the info to them and they'd provide her with the hard goods for that as well.

In other words, whatever they found that was off with the shuttles or pods that would transport the honeymooners, required her to have specific items in order to deal with what was wrong. They'd soon contact her with someone who'd make the delivery directly to her, but finding aliases that'd clear surveillance at the launch was on her. All they could do was provide the virus needed to transmit the new identities that she provided them to her wrist phone. Like she knew how to come up with stolen identities.

*Dum de doomed, dum de doomed... Oh how screwed can I get?*

It took a half hour of scrutinizing before she made her way into what appeared to be a chatter-cell with a rep for connecting buyers to sellers of anything the darkest heart desired. It was complicated to find someone who could access and sell her fake IDs. If the lines of dialogue between shopper and provider contained keywords to alert the government, she figured either the private discourse would freeze or her com-desk would blowup. Fortunately, seeing as she wasn't looking to exploit children, hire a hit, acquire a handgun or so on, it went surprisingly well.

A grueling hour after she'd been brave enough to open up to someone, they figured out helping her would potentially result in trouble for the LC. She couldn't help but chuckle when the price dropped by forty percent. Clearly others didn't like or trust the LC, either.

She finalized the transaction by sending, *yikes*, forty thousand to a site that changed IP addresses on a second-to-second basis. This was a hands-down illegal procedure, activating alarm pings on the screens of authorities. Although the funds would end up at a source no one—not even the most powerful authority—could connect with an actual name, for the rest of her life, short as that may be, she'd be tagged under a cloud of suspicion. And by the time the suits came to drag her away, they'd have a lot more concrete evidence to hang her with than a willing transfer of monies no one could prove she hadn't sent to a prince in Nigeria.

It amazed her that the United World Governments had the means to colonize past the moons of Saturn, but couldn't exterminate the guys who kept burning holes in firewalls, no matter how new or complicated.

An agonizing fifteen minutes after she'd messaged her whale-loving friends, the coordinates for a meet vanished from her screen after giving her a flash moment to read them.

*Crappin' hell.* She had to haul ass. Assuming she'd got it correct, she had less than an hour to hop two trains and find the locale in time to make the rendezvous. She knew without being told that if she was late, a paranoid guy who'd wind up behind bars for life if caught wouldn't hang about and give probable agents scrolling the Net for trouble time to zero in on him.

She ran into the bathroom, splashed water on her face and decided there was no point in wearing a hat or trying to hide her face. In for a penny, in for a pound was an ancient expression she now understood as she hurried out the door.

Fifty-some minutes and counting, she bustled herself off the train without bothering to look behind her. The street was well lit, sidewalks packed with people. Most of them headed toward the new, multi-towered cinema-mall. Holographic technology allowed individuals to project their choice onto an eight-by-ten screen that could be expanded so large it appeared to be the size of a football field, without interfering with the person seated right next to you.

The glass door to the bar beside the theater's elevators slid open at her approach. Inside, the ceiling—an enormous visual display monitor—looked like the open sky. Stars twinkled, planets in what appeared to be the far distance sparkled, and the corner of a spiral galaxy was stunningly beautiful in shades of purple, blue and black. Computer-generated music made her heartbeat pick up, her feet feel light, and if she didn't control it, her head would be bopping.

A dance floor took up most of the decadent amount of space. Singles, couples, threesomes, and—*wow*, an intense cluster of six all stepping in choreographed moments—had given in to the lure to show off in soundproof bubbles with private music controls. The contracting, warbling bubbles reacted to the dancers within, moving so they never quite touched the filmy, sparkling liquid shell no matter how robustly and powerfully athletes leaped and tossed others about within their bubbles.

Sensors clued the interior air within the bubble to bend, exerting force until the dancer either voluntarily moved or was forced out of range of another bubble or an object. Despite what looked like a valiant effort by a teenage pair of males, neither could get the other to whack into a star. She guessed any moment they'd fall flat, concussed from the pressure on their skulls and bodies the bubble pounded right back at them.

A good share of the bubbles had gone dark. Her stomach jolted as she understood the undulating movements were either gentle shows of copulation or some serious BDSM activity. Imagining the screams or gasps or orgasmic coos contained within the one jerking in a pattern of arms or torso rising and falling against a writhing base, she jerked her gaze from the dance floor to the bar.

The counter had to be forty feet long. People of all shapes, sizes and mixes of heritage clustered along it. At least she assumed they were all human, and not trained animals or robots. Hard to tell with the elaborate costumes some of them wore.

Her jaw dropped as she took in the three bartenders. Tall, wiry, long-haired males with dark blue skin — and eight arms apiece. Each guy wore a form-fitting device that completely covered the head and had six eye sockets circling the skull so they could see in all directions. It was impossible for her to tell which of their eight arms were real and which were mechanical attachments making the men look like aliens. The gorgeous server closest to her wiped the counter, made a fruity drink, set out shot glasses, filled them and scanned wrist phones as he handed out drinks — all at the same time.

A male throat cleared. "Your first time here?"

She turned to face windswept hair, dark eyes, chiseled jaw and ruffled pirate shirt open to expose his chest. The guy looked like he'd stepped off the cover of an archaic romance novel.

"Sweet chicky." His grin snaked across his face as he sidled closer. "If I buy you a bubble, will you hold it against me?"

She took a step back. "No thanks. I'm meeting someone."

"That's shiny." He winked. "Dick, I hope? Or Jane. Doesn't matter. I do either triangle." He gestured at the dance floor. "I promise to be so hot all those suckers will wish they could come a poppin' while our bubble's a rocking."

Right. She'd done her first, and most likely only, 'fast and furious' and was positive this phony would never come close to comparing. "I said no." She turned aside and startled as another man playing dress-up loomed to glower at the stud.

"She isn't the droid you're looking for," rasped Darth Vader. "Move along."

Stud laughed and muttered to her, "Your loss." He stalked off.

Darth Vader was in full costume, including the gasmask which obscured even his eyes. She hadn't needed to identify herself. Her contact would not only know what she looked like, but would have the skills to learn details down to her blood type, food preferences, and thanks to a blurry nineteenth birthday in New Orleans, that she had a mole beneath her left breast.

The guy stepped back away from the bar and gestured her to follow.

She swallowed hard and trotted up to him. "Are you…"

"Yes. Hold still." Darth Vader stopped. He took her arm with his gloved hand, touched his wrist phone to hers, sending sparks of fear into her gut, and jerked his arm aside.

He eased close, hunched, and used her to hide his arm. He removed the wrist phone he wore, took a tiny vial out of his pocket, and in a fast, deft motion sprayed the phone as it dangled between his pinched fingers.

A sharp whiff told her some sort of acid-based chemical destroyed it. He dropped what was left of the melted phone, straightened and crushed it beneath his heel, then shoved his gloved hand into his dark cloak. He pulled out a small, folded envelope, handed it to her and whispered, "Open it when you're alone. Read fast and remember. Good luck."

He spun on his large black boot heel, and headed for the exit without a backward glance. She hurried to follow. Outside, a glance to her left, right and straight up showed he'd disappeared.

On the way home, she imagined the envelope burning a hole in her small pack carefully clutched against her chest. Safety inside her apartment, every lock secured, she stood at the com-desk, took a deep breath and opened it.

Her breath caught. There was a thin bit of folded cellophane and a note, but the kind criminals had also scavenged a pair of gold wedding bands. A critical detail she hadn't thought of. Inside the bit of cellophane was a single, encapsulated pill. *Oh God.* Her stomach clenched. They'd not only found something off—it'd take drugs to deal with it?

Fingers trembling, she unfolded the paper. As soon as the air hit the ink, as fast as she could read, one by one the brief sentences, a list of instructions, faded.

*What the hell?* These anonymous hackers who'd obviously greased their way deep, quickly and efficiently into the heart of the LC hadn't found concrete proof of anything diabolical, just invoices showing purchases of some interestingly nefarious chemicals. Then, most likely using a twelve-year-old kid sitting in a cramped bedroom with an old-fashioned chart of the periodic table on the wall, paranoid minds had projected World War Two and Nazi scenarios of what those chemicals could be used for.

*Great. Tomorrow I'm gonna die.* Her role was clear and easy-peasy. Just get on a shuttle and prevent poisons from filling lungs. She tucked one of the rings and the pill inside her mini-backpack, and braced for a long and hard ponder on how she wanted to look in that body bag.

# Chapter Seven

*Will I exit this dump covered in a sheet and riding a stretcher?*

Four fifteen a.m. and Sam sat in a twenty-four-seven bar—a dive in the bowels of the city that he assumed was only frequented by masochists with a death wish or hardened males practiced at posturing the aura of gladiator to successfully repel predators.

Most of the dozen husky, heavily tattooed men sat on thick asses along the bar which was serviced by a mountain of a male with steroidal muscles that bulged and bunched beneath his leather outfit. Bearded, crusty, inked with formidable gang colors, all these guys screamed dangerous except for one. Ratty jeans studded with chains hung low on his hips, the younger man's face dripped with metal and he clung to the beefy arm of a dude the size of a tank.

*Bloody balls. What the hell have I gotten myself into?* Sam shifted uneasily on his perch in the corner booth beside the entrance slash exit and clutched the beer he had yet to taste. No way had he expected the coordinates he'd been given would lead here. He couldn't begin to imagine what the felon who'd picked this godforsaken hellhole would look like. To top it off, all he knew was his own alias was Ken, and the two-word clue he'd been given to spot his mark — think pink.

Pink. The color of chum in a place like this. He'd arrived a frantic ten minutes early, and couldn't wait to run out that door. He kept his gaze glued to the table, but his peripheral vision showed each patron checking him out. It was a matter of time before someone got in his face.

He stiffened as a Neanderthal in the center of the group, his bald head sporting the ink of the retired American flag — red, white and blue wrapped around the back of his skull from ear to ear — turned to glower at him. The guy pushed to his feet and halted as the door swung open.

Every gaze spun to the entrance. Sam felt his jaw drop, along with the rest of the testosterone-laden group, as a young woman — a teenager with powdered, alabaster skin coloring — poised in the doorway. Long blonde hair, so shiny it appeared brittle and not a strand out of place, was pulled high into a ponytail that tumbled past her hips. Inhumanly bright, eggshell-blue eyes, lashes expertly painted too black, dominated her thin face.

Pouty, scarlet red lips parted, and the tip of her tongue subtly licked along them. Sam suspected every guy there, except maybe for the gays, had dicks stiffening as they imagined pushing and pounding between those lips either for as long as that delicate, porcelain appearance could take it or until skin and bones shattered and the back of her throat gave out.

He swallowed hard and joined the rest in lowering his gaze south.

*Crap. Christ. Bullocks. The lady's here for me.* Her dress—an honest-to-fuck ball gown—was hot pink with pastel pink ruffles. A pink sash cinched round her waist that was too slender to be in proportion to such a generous bust. Swinging from one hand, she clutched a replica of herself and his heartbeat thumped as he recognized it. It was a Caucasian doll, popular in the distant past until banned by women and girls worldwide for its insipid expression and unrealistic body.

Fear scuttled down his spine as she, the woman, held the doll up and its head turned—left then right, up and down, to scan the area. The bar had fallen silent, not even a murmur. All he could hear was the clatter of keys and clanking steel as men bounced to their feet, jaws slack and eyes wide. They gawked at the woman as she stepped inside, gliding like a pro on open-toed, pink and white stilettos with tufts of pink feathers along the sides.

The worry in his gut gave way to full panic as the men reacted as a group to unglue their feet. In a mass lunge, even the bartender ran for what Sam figured was the back exit. He'd crank his neck to confirm, but that'd require him to look away from the eerie toy held by the strange woman who approached him.

Neurons snapped and crackled, telling him to get his ass in gear and follow his brothers before a ten-inch doll took off like a rocket to start chomping at his face. But, idiot that he was, he didn't move a muscle as the woman tottered closer and closer to the only fool left in the place.

"Shh," she whispered and raised her doll-free hand. A slender finger—bright pink nail polish—halted beneath his chin and pushed until he closed his mouth.

"Know who I am?" She asked in a cooing, childish voice as she laid the doll down in the center of the table and slid into the booth across from him.

"Barbie?" *Jesus, did I have to croak like a schoolboy?*

The woman laughed. "Good. And you'd be honored if I called you…?"

He cleared his throat. "Ken?" He didn't know where to look, at overflowing breasts or the doll in the process of getting to its feet to stand on the table by itself. The gaze from two pair of huge blue eyes began devouring him. His brow furrowed as the woman mirrored the doll raising its wrist phone to click a picture of his face. "Er… That thing isn't going to go for my throat, is it?"

The woman's painted face went blank. "Do as I say or you'll pray my pet aims that high. Understand?" Her soft voice had hardened, that false soprano gone.

His balls tingled. "Yes, ma'am." He fought to stay in his seat as the doll perched its hands on its hips and the head tipped back and rotated full circle. "What—"

"Shut up and listen," the woman snapped. "Security cams and vid-feed will only be blocked for five. Give me your arm."

He shifted to the side, avoiding the doll as he slapped his arm across the table.

"Just hold still." The woman laid her wrist phone over his stolen one, and surprise gave way to hopeless resignation. He'd paid what had to be the most conspicuous criminal in the world to download these programs that'd link a beaten and bound man's identification to Sam's genetic profile. All threads thought of, including pics changed on any site the pilot had ever used with one of Sam. Costly yet simplistic to erase a man's existence and replace him with someone else. The doll poised, hands on tiny hips, head slowly rotating as her freaky gaze continued to scan the empty bar.

Speaking of the mass exodus. "Why'd everyone run like that?"

The woman's eyes couldn't get any larger. "You're a cutie, aren't you, Kenny-boy?" She leaned closer. "All citizens of the United Worlds understand it's wrong, deadly wrong, to tamper with security. Any bad boy who hasn't lived under a rock in the past few months knows if they're recorded in the presence of a" — she winked — "tool that's six to ten inches long, has thin to thick girth, and a pretty head that can screw with cams — it's an automatic life sentence."

She separated their wrist phones. Her slender fingers stroked along his arm before gesturing at the camera above the mirror behind the bar.

His breath caught as the implication of what she said sank in. Even if he, the established pilot of a shuttle, left now, raced to dodge the security rushing to their locale as this strange creature calmly sat licking her lips and seductively grinning at him, he'd be nailed along with the rest of the poor sods who'd left full drinks all along the bar. There'd be no chance to get on that shuttle — his life thrown away for nothing.

He jerked his arm up and glanced at the screen on his wrist phone. The transaction was completed. Thirty grand had left his account for another's. "Great. Thanks. But I hadn't expected my face over the Net this evening. Tomorrow, maybe." Rage reared, bile splashing up into his throat. Surely he had a minute or two left. Plenty of time to smash a doll and strangle a woman.

*Not a killer, are you, asshole? Get the fuck out of here.* He shoved to his feet and froze as he saw the doll had moved. It now stood in front of him.

"Have some trust, sweetheart." The woman stood as well, stepping out of the booth. "It's not your *actual* face that'll surf the cyber-wave." She came round to take his arm as the doll rose from the level of his waist up into the air to halt inches from his face. The doll's eyes shuttered open and closed. As it floated back down, the woman released Sam and grabbed it.

"For a dick pretending to be an androgynous Ken, you did terrible." The woman smiled, glancing at his crotch. "If you'd show off that package I think you have, they'll never believe the images now ingrained into time-sensitive frames of those security cams."

He gulped. "Huh? I'm not being recorded? The image of a toy is?"

She giggled. "Gosh, you're cute. I love it when a man isn't a total dummy." The woman hurried as fast as those heels would allow toward the door. "Nice doing business with you. Best run before the powers-that-be wake up to the fact you're not the doll you appear to be, and they come hunting a hot, manly man about to power up a rocket for the moon." She paused to toss him a wink and eyeballed his crotch again. "If I didn't swing the other way, I'd hop on that stick. You seem like a genuinely nice guy. Good luck."

He cocked his head, gaze on her swaying butt as she exited, and shuddered. Thank Christ for lesbians. He had no desire to get any closer than he already had to a female genetically enhanced to look like that. Not while he had a true beauty of a pretend-hooker to fantasize about.

*Bloody balls, asshole. Hurry after that damn doll before you're in prison surrounded by guys.*

He went for the full-out run and burst out of the door. He continued running past unlit, spaced poles with cams attached to them that may or may not work, toward a small group of people. He shot a glance over his shoulder, and relief filled his lungs as he saw nothing on his heels. One block then two, and he slowed to close in on five guys.

"Wait up," he called out. "That you, Bruce?"

The men stopped.

"Oh. Sorry. Thought I knew you." He kept walking.

"Yo. Man — not a good place to stroll alone," one of them said. "Most the cams here look like they're out."

Sam knew that didn't mean security wouldn't swarm the area shortly. It'd just be after his wrist phone was gone and the blood from his slit throat had cooled.

"Spot us a C and we'll walk you to the train," called out another.

A measly hundred dollars? *Hell, yeah.* He halted. "How far?"

"Three blocks."

Sam pushed up his sleeve, exposing the stolen wrist phone he wore. He swallowed hard as a stranger's ID — Roger Moore, the pilot whom he'd bashed unconscious, lit the corner of the screen. He made sure his face remained expressionless and tapped his bank code in. "That'd be great." He gestured the first man closer. He'd have paid ten times that without blinking an eye.

A hurried and awkward walk later, Sam mumbled, "Thanks," to the group surrounding him and slunk ahead for the westbound train. The adrenaline rush of surviving Miss Pink had worn off, leaving his limbs heavy and sluggish. He had one more stop before he could head back and catch a couple of hours of sleep. Just his luck, a glance on the Net showed him there was a Walled-Market in the area. Open twenty-four-seven, and par for the course, the mega-outlet store filled with crap sweltering under rows of cheap, old-fashioned fluorescent lighting that made him want to gouge his eyes out, was in the opposite direction. He hurried.

No surprise, but the store was almost empty of items and customers. A big 'Going Out of Business' sign hung in the front window. No one with scruples concerning the planet ever went here. Most of the world shopped online, and he was amazed these last dinosaurs clung on as long as they had.

It didn't take long to comb through the disheveled racks. He settled on a small drill, hammer and an ice pick. Despite only two other men in the place, the damn automated checkout took forever to scan his wrist phone. He'd have been paranoid, but the guy in the exit grid alongside him was pounding his fist on the scanner and swearing. He finally unclenched his jaws when he sat on the train again, no one paying any attention to him.

Back at his lair, he got right to it. Sam wasn't inept with mechanical skills, but the ice pick was worthless, the hammerhead snapped off and it took an arm-numbing five minutes of drilling and a destroyed drill bit before the tiny case popped open.

The air in his lungs froze. Alongside clips of ammo, one legal-for-pilots handgun and coiled tripwire that'd slice a throat, lay five tiny pieces of what he assumed could be screwed together into a micro, easily concealed in one hand assault weapon that included a laser point scope for precision firing.

A search online showed him comparable weapons. All highly illegal worldwide, for police as well as civilians—mandatory death penalty without appeal if fired and life sentence if caught with even one of the parts. The weapon could be used within a closed aircraft without affecting stability or compromising the hull integrity, unless fired repeatedly into it. Minus the easily attachable scope, the .9 kilogram monster could fit in a child's palm. The Net told him the device, labeled The Devil's Dick or a DD, was capable of firing a hundred pea-sized bullets per clip. Each expanded upon impact to ensure maximum damage to organic structures and certain death if but one pea penetrated major organs.

He swallowed hard, pocketed the handgun able to fire a measly thirty rounds per clip of non-exploding ammo and shoved the case beneath a floorboard inside the closet. A moment later he was stripped down in the shower, the hottest water he could manage drilling on his skin trying—and losing—to cease the thoughts of the harm such a weapon could do to a man within a rocket hurtling through space.

# Chapter Eight

Jenna stood in the shower, trembling. Hot water had pounded on her back for some time now, but she still couldn't stop shaking. She'd done the unthinkable and had to pull herself together in order to deal with the buzz soon to come at her door.

Oh God—how could she be so...risqué? Waste any amount of what little money was left that Sam had given her. For what possible reason, assuming she didn't get popped the moment she approached the shuttle so that no one but morgue employees would know what she'd done, could she expect Sam Dexter would want a second helping? A more prolonged one that'd involve clothing coming off?

Odds were Sam had smoothed things over with the goddess at the bar. He'd have run his fingers along the woman's slender arm, rested his other hand dangerously high on her thigh, bent to her ear and murmured magic. The uptight beauty queen would have melted, and slipped her manicured fingers into his hand as he convinced her that the short, disheveled slut who'd scurried out of the bar was a nobody he'd barely touched and wanted nothing more to do with.

*'Never contact me again. Stay out of bars and far away from me.'*

Jenna's fingers clenched and the bodywash lurched out of her hand. She barely felt the micro-thin tube whack her on the toes as thoughts ran wild, stirring her anxieties into a tempest no teapot of a frazzled mind could contain for long without going mad. *Hellsbells. I'm acting like a teenager.* She heaved a sigh and tapped the five minute cool down then shut-off for the water, wishing she could turn off the spiral of insecurity as easily.

After telling his fiancée what she needed to know to help him save lovers worldwide, Sam would have whisked the woman home to their bed. Then, come morning, to follow their full moonlit night of more passion any girl had a right to be entitled to — *was he on top, alongside, behind, beneath her right now?* — he'd escort his purring bride to the shuttle.

Once the image of Sam Dexter went live over the Net as a hero, the pair would flee to the most erotic honeymoon suite Earth had to offer, paid for courtesy of billions of admirers. He'd sweep his bride, dressed in swirls of white, up into his arms while grateful families clapped and cheered. In the room, he'd kick the door closed with his heel and undress his bride slowly, pin her down and work that thick, skilled cock into the luckiest woman alive for hours of intense lovemaking. Any fleeting memory of a five-minute screw in a public restroom would be long gone. He'd occasionally think of Jenna as that hooker whose name he didn't know, the fool who'd showed up at the launch as an unneeded, unwanted, ignored third wheel.

*I'm such an idiot.*

*Yeah, well, so what. I'm involved, whether the perfect couple wants it or not.*

She pushed her sleep-deprived body out of the shower and stood on the vent centered in front of the mirror. A tap of her finger to the side of the sink activated the dryapp. The tube came down, and a couple of toasty minutes later, water drops had evaporated from head to toe.

The moment she stepped away from the sink to wrap a robe around her, the com buzzed and her stomach roiled. The easy part was finished. Now she needed the balls to deal with the other insanity she'd ordered up. Legs shaking, she headed out of the bathroom and tapped the link on the com-desk. "Is this...the Love Center Rep?"

"Yes. Open up before I get mugged."

Her breath froze when she heard the voice. She swallowed hard, struggling for more than a squeak to pass her lips. "Um...I expected a woman."

"Listen, dearie, if you don't let me in, it won't matter what gender I am. I'll be against the wall out here with my pants down. You can't leave merchandise this dangerous standing in a dank corridor..."

*Why, oh why did I do this?* The man grumbled on while she tightened the belt round her waist and dragged her feet to open the door a crack. Her heartbeat stopped. The guy — a representative who supposedly provided an expensive service sponsored by the LC — was the most attractive and scariest thing she'd ever seen as he shoved his open-toed sandaled foot — with sparkly, iridescent nail polish, laced in thin red straps — against the door to force his way in.

A full-length, hooded black duster folded on his arm and a large sky-blue bag in hand, the man stood half a foot taller than her. Soft purple hair with pink highlights floated about his muscled frame. He blinked at her where she was rooted to the floor and allowed her a chance to gawk as a smirk played about his lips.

Pulled into four, loosely plaited pigtails, his glistening hair tumbled to his knees. He'd look effeminate if not for his lean face, masculine jaw, thick brows and the intricate blue and green inked vines running from his cheekbones, curling around his neck and into the sapphire leather shirt glued to a sculpted chest. Black pants hugged his groin, advertising what promised to be all male, no enhancements.

The guy was gorgeous and his smug grin told her he knew that he had her heart racing. She flinched. "Listen. There's been a mistake. I didn't…shouldn't have called you."

He stared at her from sparkling, violet eyes and she tumbled into them. "There, there. Don't be afraid of me, sister. I'm here to help." He raked his intense gaze over her and his smile widened. "Sweet. You'll be an easy fix."

He hustled farther inside, turned to push the door closed, giving her a glimpse of an exquisite backside. He shrugged the duster and bag to the floor. "My time with you must be hurried. I've worked all night and thank the stars and full moon, you're my last. This city was in a panic." He winked at her. "You'd think a hundred couples or more were off on honeymoons or something."

"But I-I changed my mind. I'll pay—"

Two steps forward and his hand shot out to snag the front of her robe. "Don't panic, dearie. I just want to do you and go home. You'd best be ready under this." Her mouth fell open as his other hand got in on the action, jerking at the belt. Before her nervous yelp cleared her throat, the robe puddled around her feet and she stood nude before him. He eased back, eyeballing her hands flying to cover her crotch. He tsked. "Stop that. You're exquisite. Almost perfect. I'll make you so pretty his...it is a he, right? His head will never stop spinning."

She gulped. "Really?"

"Oh yes. But in all honesty, my head's in a whirl with you just as you are, so lovely and committed to a partner that isn't *moi*. Hm...too bad my guy isn't into foursomes. The poor thing can barely handle a ménage." The man's charming giggle dissolved her fear as he spun round to grab the bag, then his strong hand clasped her elbow. She drew in a deep breath of lilacs as he marched her into the bedroom, his extravagant hair swirling in a tangle of purple and pinks as it kissed his long legs.

"Hope you don't mind the cut and shave in here, sweet thing, instead of the bathroom. I'd rather work with some elbow room. Can you imagine? They say the mansions on Mars have three bathrooms, including a master shower that'd hold an orgy." He pushed her to sit down on the bed, pulled her hand out and ran his fingers up and down her arm. "Get used to my touch, dearie. I'm going places only your lovers have been — oh yes I am. Just relax. My name's Laven or Lav or Lavender. Lenard Harding if you're pissed at me. And, Miss Last But Not Least on my schedule, what's your real name?"

"Jenna..."

Time flew by in a daze of sitting, standing, legs spread wide. She'd never had anyone spruce her up like this, let alone a man who guaranteed she'd not look at purple the same way again. Lav's touch, his hands, were enchanting. A flawless tactile experience of a confident guy, without a hint of embarrassment or seduction. The jitters had a heyday inside her chest when he tied the last thread round her leg, pulled her to her feet and twirled her about.

"Oh damn it, dearie. I need the coldest of showers. I have to wrap myself in my duster to hide my gun as it is. It's going to be a painful ride home."

Her gaze flitted down to his crotch and she smiled. That bulge was lovely but not indecent.

He tilted his head, pretending her attention hadn't left his bright eyes and his hand flew to his mouth. "Oh yessss. You sure about the pink and lime exotic lace teddy instead of the Dominatrix whip pattern? Makes me want to cuddle you, not get on my knees and beg you to ravish me."

She managed a shaky nod and he laughed. "Okay. Doesn't matter what you pick. He's going to think that shuttle went off course and he's landed in heaven. Never had a girl fill out any type of lingerie like you." He grinned and patted his chest over his heart. "Glad you're headed to the moon. When your man keels over from a heart attack, you won't be able to come crying to me."

She shivered, basking in the attention of the cheerful flirt who knew her every dimple. The camisole he'd poured her into was pretty much made out of lines of fabric. A cobweb of expensive silk that supported her breasts while leaving their front and nipples exposed. The lace-edged hem brushed the top of her groin and the curve of her butt cheeks, the center of her butt was exposed as an open circle, tied in place by ink-black straps hugging round the top of her legs.

Lav had insisted she not leave any part of her bottom uncovered. Below the camisole, she wore teeny-tiny hot pink French panties with rip-away sides, and beneath that a sparkly red thong. The luxurious strip of fabric teased and caressed where Lav had trimmed and shaped her pubic hair instead of shaving her. He'd said the craze for the childish look was outdated. That the unscented crème conditioner he used would make her so deliciously soft and refined, yet divinely au natural, he doubted a lover would ever stop kissing her, no matter how many times her own cream added flavor.

"Oh God. I feel…"

Lav smacked a kiss on her forehead. "You feel and smell damn sexy. Cinnamon, vanilla and almond, laced with the scent of an aroused damsel is a seductive combo I only give to the sweetest of girls." He bent to her ear. "Call me if your intended doesn't treat you right. I'll fly to any satellite in any galaxy for you, love." He straightened and began stuffing rejected undergarments back in his bag. He gestured to the tube of conditioner and small vial of perfume still on the bed. "Not that you, dearie, needed either, but keep those. I'll say I left them by accident."

"Oh no. You could get in trouble."

He winked, shouldering the bag. "That's my lover's name. Hopefully I'll soon do just that and more than once, from many angles, and I'll forget all about lovely ladies. Thanks for making a long night fun and make sure you—" He dropped the bag. Those gorgeous violet eyes narrowed. "I don't trust you, sister. What are you wearing to the launch?"

"Er… In the closet."

Lav strode to the closet, flung the door open and pulled out the crisp sky-blue button-down top with matching knee-length skirt and zippered sides. "Perfect. Quaint and begging to be removed." He mock scowled at her. "Put it on. Now. So I know you'll be less apt to mess with my masterpiece."

Ten minutes later, she stood in her doorway, fully dressed, watching Lav blow her a kiss from the elevator. As the door closed on him, her smile ran for the hills and she slipped back inside and locked the door.

Lav seemed to have a kind heart and he certainly was a pro — touched her with sureness and no sexual heat, a job he'd done a million times. He'd noticed errant hairs, but not seen past the mask beneath the makeup he'd expertly applied to her face. He thought her nothing but a skittish girl who'd stayed up all night because she yearned to excite the man who'd given her a ring.

Part of that was right. She was a criminal who'd gone without sleep to meet with terrorists, and oh God, did she hunger to please a specific man. Lusted and longed for the chance to entice a famous bachelor who'd handed a ring to another and told the unexpected quickie never to contact him again, let alone show up with a pair of rings neither one of them had chosen.

*Who am I kidding?* Jenna ran her fingers through her exquisitely trimmed hair, freshly shampooed and no color or glitter added because Lav had cooed over her natural locks. Even if Sam Dexter arrived without a bride — doing something insanely stupid like pretending to be a pilot — and even if he saw her at all and went along with her equally insanely stupid plan, and even if they walked onto that shuttle together, he'd either not care or not get a chance to go beyond the prim blouse and schoolmarm skirt.

She clenched her groin muscles, feeling the thong rub in a mockery of not even close to comparing to what Sam's fingers had done in a hot few minutes.

*Even ifs be damned. I feel pretty — really pretty — and no matter what happens, I'll get a chance to see him.*

# Chapter Nine

*Thank whoever the patron saint of martyrs is that I'll never see my true-love-fantasy-girl again.* Limbs heavy, feet concrete, vodka and no sleep fueling his last night on Earth, it felt like nothing but short-circuiting wires powered Sam's sluggish brain. *Fuckin' hell.* He was an imposter about to hijack a shuttle. An act labeled terrorism, which was surely more despised and ruthlessly punished than ethnic cleansing of fertile humans. And what type of crackpot accuses governments of potential mass murder with no concrete evidence other than gut instinct, and one pervert of a pilot with a cracked skull who'd had a horrendous weapon of mass destruction in his apartment? Now, insanely, stashed in a place coated with Sam's fingerprints? Falsified records only postponed the inevitable. All authorities had to do was grab hold of Moore's fingers and Sam's and the gig was up.

*What if I'm wrong?*

*Then you're a dead man, asshole.*

*What if I'm right?*

*Then you're a dead man, asshole.*

*What if I... Shut up and get on with this.*

The pilot-legal handgun tucked to his back under the pressed pilot jacket, Sam strode with false confidence past the rows of couples. He could feel their gazes burning into his backside as he approached the shuttle. Someone was certain to cry out any second, calling for security to apprehend a fraud who knew as much about flying a rocket as websites could cram into a guy within two days of losing a bride.

"Sweetheart, over here," called a low soprano. "Sam? You need to wait in line with me."

*That's my name, but sweetheart?* No woman had ever called him that before. More importantly, his gut clenched because the voice sounded hauntingly familiar.

*Don't look. Can't be.* He kept walking.

"You bastard, quit messin' around."

He came to a dead stop. Bastard was an endearment he'd heard countless times.

"Sam? Please."

He turned and it felt like his heart hit the pavement. The woman he'd obsessed about non-stop for forty-eight hours stood alone, a little backpack on her shoulder, almost at the end of the queue.

*Oh shit.* His heartbeat skipped, his cock perked and he sucked in a sharp inhalation. Songbirds would return to spin round his head, if they weren't being blasted out of existence by shock and a bunch more words that began with 'S'. *She's here!* Too short, too sexy, too smart, but, without doubt, love at second sight. *Christ, she's so sweet.* Her presence, doing the one thing he'd told her not to do, could be a good thing, right?

*Hell, no. I'll kill her myself.* He stomped forward with the fury of a guy worried the only woman he'd ever thought of as a sweetheart would never squirm with joy against anyone's chest again, let alone his.

"Have you been drinking?" She blushed at him. "Silly man. That pilot jacket won't fool anyone. But geez, you do look handsome." Her gaze fell, bright eyes glistening, as she babbled. "Wow. Can't believe we're headed on our honeymoon and I'm so nervous. Do stop playing around. Okay, husband?"

Sam stopped, toe-to-toe with her. His hand beneath her chin forced her to face his most ferocious scowl. "It's almost as if I don't even know your name, wife." *Ohgodohgod, she's not a hallucination. So pretty. Smells so damn good. Want to hug, kiss… Can't.* He dropped his hand, making sure she noted his fingers curling into a fist. "Didn't you get the message when justice said honor and obey? I told—"

"Stop being mean." She glanced down at her mid-calf skirt. "I know you wanted me to wear that black thing. Short skirts get me into so much trouble. We must behave, or they'll throw us out the airlock."

She reached for him and his hand shot out so fast to grab hold of hers, an adorable twitch of a smile curved her lips. "You missed me then?"

*Absolutely. Like I'd found and lost a part of my soul.* He deepened his frown to an intense glower. "No. I said no. I'm afraid—"

"Yes. I said yes and I'm not afraid." The timid edge about her disappeared, eaten up by defiance. "What could you possibly fear so much you snuck off on this morning, of all days?"

Her little fingers trembled in his, and he grumbled, "I only had a few beers. Forgive me? You're the best quickie to ever happen to me. But if you're as smart as I think you are, nothing like someone stupid enough to hook up with random guys, you'll divorce me right now."

He narrowed his eyes at the pair behind them. They turned to each other, pretending they weren't listening.

"Never. Till death do us part." She tugged her hand from his and he reluctantly let go, watching her open the pack.

"You left your ring on the dresser," she said. "I finished and filed the paperwork as well. Isn't it stupid we still call it paperwork, when no trees are...?" She drew in a deep breath and peeked at him. "Sorry. I'll stop babbling any time now. Regardless, we're all set, Mister Bond." She glanced at the woman in front. "Good thing he's so darn cute, right?"

His jaw twitched. What the hell had she done? And why couldn't he stop staring at the splash of freckles across her face, those sweet lips, the dip in her throat he'd savored when he'd kissed the spot, the swell of breasts within the button-down blouse and pebbled nipples he hadn't tasted?

"Here you go, Samuel James Bond." She pressed a thin gold band into his hand that matched the one gleaming on her finger, angling her wrist phone screen for him. *Jenna Bond.* He licked his lips and jerked his attention back to face, breasts, stomach, heaven, long...short legs.

*Christ, not good.* She was trembling. Nervous and afraid, a strong breeze could topple her. Unlike his normal type where he had but to turn his head and dip an inch or so to reach lips, he'd love to grab her and pull her to tiptoes, and bend—*behave, asshole.* Felt like his heart plummeted to his damn toes. He had to protect her—from boarding that shuttle and from himself.

"Hm, notice the witnesses?" she mumbled. "Stop looking at me like that."

"No. It's as if I never had chance to really look at a gift that I have to return." He continued raking his gaze over her. "Speaking of cute butts. Turn round. Run home and make sure we didn't leave a light on."

She snorted. "Ha ha. A check of home security is easy enough from here. Let me show you how couples save the day... I mean, don't waste electricity by cooperating." She grabbed his wrist and linked her phone to his. Electricity jolted up his arm, racing in every direction before his brain kicked in and rerouted the current to skip north, east and west to concentrate on south.

His eyes widened, hairs on his arms competing with the rest of him to stiffen, as she unhooked their phones and playfully slapped his stomach. "Everything's fine. Forget the past and pay attention to the now. It's almost time to board."

Attention? Yeah, that wasn't an issue. His cock was as hard as it had been when he'd seen her for the first time two days ago. He'd gone past high alert into ramrod mode, more than eager to salute her over and over for hours, days, years — a lifetime.

"Sam?" Her voice quavered.

He shook his head, jarring the layer of lust swamping him. Maybe she wasn't trying to prove to him again how magnetically attracted they were. She wanted him to understand authorities would connect her to him, the man with a handgun registered to the guy bound and gagged and laid out on his bed. The idiot who had to get rid of his unexpected wife and get onboard that shuttle as an employee loaded with something other than a throbbing hard-on, ready to pilot newlyweds into the stars.

But, Christ. She — *my wife!* — had gone viral with her identity. Her alias was now connected to him. Making her, this sweetheart of a spy — *Bond, lol* — as doomed as he was. It also meant that whatever she'd done to his wrist phone guaranteed them access into the shuttle, if some numbnut wasn't carrying a stolen weapon or a real co-pilot came running out to replace the missing one.

Few techies knew how to override files, let alone replace them so thoroughly security couldn't tell. But what if he was wrong? Could be she'd done nothing but further sabotage a fool's mission. Nah, that didn't ring right. Despite only knowing Mrs. Bond in the biblical sense, he was certain the beauty staring up at him all starry-eyed was the real deal. A brilliant, highly motivated do-gooder about to regret he wasn't up to par, not even close.

She smiled at him, taking in the pilot cap. "I can't believe you dressed as if you could drive that thing. You're going into a pod like your wife is, got it?"

*Fuck no.* His jaw clenched, heart pounding. He didn't seem able to think much past how much he wanted to grasp her and take those lips he'd never expected to see again.

*Do it. We're newlyweds. Who's gonna care if I kiss and kiss and fuck…make love to her mouth with my tongue.*

*Forget it, you sick dog. Keep your tongue on lockdown, swallow that drool and save her.*

Somehow he had to keep this Mata Hari grounded — her feet firmly planted and heading anywhere but outer space. Not like she knew he'd get busted with a handgun if he walked up the steps with the rest of the passengers. Anxiety galloped in his veins as the surroundings closed in around him. Eight more couples, and their turn to extend wrist phones while being rayed for metal and plastic. He snapped his gaze back to her.

Jenna. A lovely name, maybe even real. What had she said? That he was going into a pod like her? He furrowed his brow. "Lonely souls destined for a jail cell do whatever shenanigans they damn well please, little lady. Those pods are no fun. Only room for one, my dear. That's clearly written in the stars."

"Little? No way. I can't associate you, *my dear*, with the word little." Heat flooded her cheeks. "Have to wait until we get to the moon. Then we can do any shenanigans," she smirked. "Seriously, who says that? Then we can do whatever you…I mean, that *I* want."

He plastered on a leer. "Wrong. I'm not a patient guy. Forget the out-of-the-atmosphere-high club. I'm primed and ready and dangerously *illegal*." He clasped her arms, yanked her forward, and pressed his groin into her stomach. "You're a sweet patsy who's gonna get screwed. Again. Run fast, *little girl*, from a Casanova, Bluebeard, Henry the VIII who marries in a blink of an eye, and doesn't even remember it."

She punched him in the chest, exaggerated a wince, and squirmed away. "Stop that. Don't you understand what happened? Any identity you think you have, Mister Womanizer who's really not a rake but…pardon more lame literary puns…a dark and stormy knight on a quest that must have two rings, not one, to bind them all. Stupid Samwise Gamgee, all that you were was erased when you signed that 'until death do us part' doc. We are *both* headed for Mount Doom…I mean Mons Hadley — the lunar crater waiting for bonded partners to explore. So shut up about divorce or single status or…just shut up."

*Fuckin' balls.* She'd erased his stolen pilot clearance? His jaw clenched so hard his teeth ached. "Woman…Jenna, do you know what you've done?" *Should I kiss her or strangle her?*

"I do. I've landed the hottest guy on Earth who can't conceal a smokin' pistol, not from me." Her smile slipped, her voice lowered to a mumble. "Do you think bad things happen to those who hesitate?" She inched closer. "That I should be bold and go where all those ex-wives have gone while I still can?"

She slipped her hand beneath his jacket and his cock began humming, sucking down every drop of blood left in his brain. Last time she'd worked her hand beneath his shirt... Damn it, those clever fingers headed the wrong direction. He grunted as he felt her hand bump into the revolver. Shrugging the opened pack to her arm, she flung her other arm around him, and his insane dick cheered as she fumbled her hand over his butt.

He bent to growl in her ear. "Leave it. I can talk my way out of anything." Public indecency... They'd get tasered before they even boarded the death shuttle.

"Right. Dumbass."

He snorted while she wiggled the handgun loose. "Leave the dumbass then. The real action is round front anyway." The couples, only three of them now, looked anywhere but at them.

"Later. We'd best aim to misbehave on another world." Jenna eased the weapon out and around. "Too many eyes on this one." The slight smack to his drooling cock wasn't necessary but it — almost — helped him deflate as she shoved the revolver into the pack. Her face as red as the highlights in her bright hair, she rummaged through the bag. She pulled her clenched fist out, as if she held something the size of a button, and awkwardly closed the pack.

He grabbed for it.

"No." She swung it from him. "Pay attention. You can rip straps, so fate rests with you after we board." Big, brown, most frightened of eyes pleaded with him. "Trust me?" Her hand flew to her mouth then reached out to him. "Give me a kiss?"

*What's she up to?* She looked so worried.

Ahh, hell. Moth to flame, bee to honey, husband to wife, he homed in.

He was vaguely aware of the final couple shuffling around them. He was completely aware of her tongue insisting he swallow the fat pill she slipped from her mouth into his.

The moment his Adam's apple bobbed, she broke the kiss. "Not sure," she whispered, "but a guy I hired found invoices. Chemicals. Pharmaceuticals. I think...hope you swallowed the antidote."

"Jenna and Samuel Bond?" a rough male voice bellowed.

Sam turned. A brute wearing an attendant's uniform, LC on the lapel, glowered at them.

The bastard ogled Jenna. "Save it for the moon. Lucky I don't have you arrested for overly annoying public displays of affection." The man shifted his gaze to Sam and narrowed his eyes. "Nice suit coat and hat." He flipped his fingers at the shuttle. "As if any pretty flyboy compensating for a"—his tones flooded with sarcasm—"wittle itty dick would handle one of these."

Sam swallowed his snort. Doomed regardless, before he went down perhaps he'd have chance to shove the pilot cap down this prick's throat.

The guy glowered right back at him and snapped, "Move your horny ass or this trip of a lifetime leaves without you."

Mister Customer Service—who needed his face rearranged—disappeared into the shuttle. Approaching footsteps had Sam twisting his head to the side. A thin, short man in need of a shave thrust his arm into a white jacket identical to the one Sam wore, while striding in a beeline for the separate entrance to the cockpit.

Christ. Calling in a sub, instead of delaying and investigating what happened to the scheduled pilot, sure didn't bode well for any sucker boarding this ride to the moon. Also incriminating, what legitimate pilot could they get with such short notice, and why was no one asking who the clown was standing in line wearing a uniform, as if he should be called into action?

He was screwed. Royally. The only hope to make the brutal beating in store for him tolerable was to get it through the thick head of his bride that she didn't have to be on the rack with him.

He turned to stare at the woman on his arm. Jenna was so beautiful and so stupid for trying to help him. *Want you, think I love you, have to lose you. Bye, sweetheart.* He smacked a kiss on her forehead. "Honeymoon's over. Go home." He growled, knocked her hand from him and hurried for the ramp.

He groaned as she ran on his heels. He slowed, readying to force the pack from her as their feet hit the ramp. Little minx anticipated, swerving aside.

He understood his little minx was a genius as the pack dropped from her fingers. She stumbled, kicking it beneath the shuttle, and he grasped her arm. "Easy, sweetheart. Walk up the ramp, not around it."

She pulled her arm free and grabbed to clutch his hand, holding on like a petrified child. "I'm glad you're not clumsy," she mumbled. "My left knee gives out. Think about that — I mean me, my literary genius — when they close that lid."

She'd drugged him with something and it fell on him to be the hero? Fine. But he needed more of a clue than think of dimpled knees hidden by that long skirt. Their wrist phones cleared and his heartbeat returned. The still-scowling brute didn't speak, gesturing them to enter the aisle.

Rows of pods, lids closed on all but the end pair closest to the cockpit. A solid-looking attendant blocked the cockpit, and Brute walked behind Sam's bride — *I wish* — otherwise, no one else was still standing in the hundred foot long aisle. Damn, wouldn't he have at least a few minutes to figure out the scam before they went into the sky?

He tugged Jenna until they reached the open pods, stopped and cleared his throat. "Hang on a moment. I have to speak to the pilots. It's important."

Goons burst out laughing. "Don't be a pansy." The closer guy moved in on Sam. "If you piss yourself, we'll hose you down on the moon."

"No. Listen—" *Watch out, incoming.* A large fist connected with his jaw. *Fuckin' take it, hero.* He absorbed the blow without a stumble, his arm raised.

Jenna's yelp, her hand ripping from his, froze his fist. He turned. Brute had her in a chokehold.

"In the pod, loverboy, before I snap her pretty neck," Brute said.

*Idiot, idiot, idiot.* He should have known more than the pilots would be a part of this. His hesitation, and a punch to his kidney, cost him his feet. The second goon whacked him on the back and muscled him into the pod. He managed one deep inhalation before the lid came down.

Darkness.

Barely a minute and the feel of rushing, rushing — airborne.

He yawned. *Jesus, what's wrong with me? That bastard manhandled Jenna and I'm fine with taking a nap?*

Fear began racing up his spine as he came to panicked deductions. He'd been drugged. His lungs didn't work right, that's why he was fighting another yawn. Too bad he didn't know what else the pill Jenna had given him did, other than make him feel like an elephant sat on his chest.

Fuck, forget the pill. What was *he* supposed to do?

A red light flickered in the far left corner.

A shallow breath and his lungs immobilized.

Sudden eureka had him scared shitless. Activated by something seeping into this sealed pod, the pill he'd swallowed had made his lungs literally lock. He couldn't inhale if he wanted to, and he was fairly certain lives depended on him not breathing in the toxic air. Assuming Jenna was either the chemical mastermind he thought her to be or had gotten expert help, the drug controlling his respiration would wear off before brain death. That meant he had three to five minutes to escape—less if he expected to save anyone other than his own sorry ass.

*Balls.* His arms strapped, he couldn't unclip the harness. That's why she'd delegated to him. It took all his strength, fingernails cracked and bleeding, to gain his limbs.

*Goddamn balls.* Lid didn't budge.

He threw himself upward. Came down so hard his brain rattled and a thought jarred loose. A soft voice floated from memory, "*my left knee gives out*". Literary genius? Gives out—get out? Had she hired some geek extraordinaire or was she the genius who burned through serious encryptions and walls to glimpse schematics of these blasted coffins? Figured out what gas they'd use and how to counteract it, so at least one victim remained conscious?

*Please, please, let it be so.* He raised his hand, felt along the left edge and hope flared.

His knuckle scrapped raw, but he managed to slide the thin lever. He cracked the lid enough to roll out, staggered onto his feet, and allowed the lid to slam closed before too much poisoned gas seeped out.

Dark clouds edged his vision as he scanned the aisle, legs wobbling like a lamb going to slaughter, to see no lurking forms. Thank Christ, the goons must be in the cockpit. Now if only his lungs would begin to work.

They didn't.

Not until he'd opened Jenna's pod, lifted her limp body out, dropped her in the aisle and yanked two unconscious men and another woman from their coffins did the blackness force him to his knees. Finally his chest heaved, drawing in the only-mildly tainted air that spilled out when he'd opened the pods, into his lungs.

His head swam, but he remained upright. The poison injected into each pod had to have been a measured burst, dissipating upon opening, or he'd be lying flat instead of swallowing back vomit.

He wiped his mouth and hustled. A sharp smack to each face brought survivors round. They freed four men, five women then eight lifeless bodies. It became clear to Sam that too much time had passed. They'd be allowing the sweet smelling gas that remained inside the pods to escape if they opened the rest, who likely — because of the fate that had already befallen passengers in the last eight pods they'd opened — to find no pulse.

Of course guilt shook him when one of the ashen-faced men found another guy breathing. He was almost too busy to care as he held a vomiting Jenna. The rescuer stared back at him, tears on his cheeks, standing beside a pod without a stirring body lying outside it.

The survivors who weren't vomiting checked the remaining pods, trying not to inhale as they felt for a pulse, then slammed lids closed.

The name of the man who'd lost his bride was Kurt. A big guy, Kurt's closed fisted blow to Brute's face as he opened the cockpit door pretty near took Brute's head off. Twist to the neck, thud to the floor told Sam he was dead. No dummy, Kurt bent over the guy and straightened with a weapon—a nice-sized Glock—in hand.

Once they'd subdued the other attendant and both pilots, and had the three strapped and locked inside foul-smelling but survivable pods now that they'd been aired out, Sam and Kurt re-entered the cockpit. They'd left Jenna explaining to the grief-stricken honeymooners, including one man he rather wished they'd imprison in a pod. He didn't like the way the guy gawked at Jenna who was ignoring him. Instead she looked to Sam, insisting along with the rest of the handful of survivors that the fraud in the uniform should take the wheel.

Kurt stumbled into the cockpit on Sam's heels. "I never killed anyone before." The guy swiped at his cheeks, angrily wiping tears. "Never seen a bunch of murdered people to include my wife, either. This is beyond sick." He dropped into the copilot seat and his chest heaved. "Know how to fly a lunar shuttle?"

Sam stared into the wild blue yonder. "How hard can it be?"

"Guess we're all dead." Kurt glared at the complicated instrument dashboard.

"Beyond sick is right." Sam swallowed against the bitter taste of cooling adrenaline. "So much more devious than I ever feared. But when planning mass murder, why go to the expense to actually build rockets? These shuttles must be nothing but winged gas chambers, hopefully still on autopilot."

"Yeah. That makes sense. I noticed in the last pod I opened on a dead woman—she was a tiny thing— there's grooves cut in a rectangular pattern in the base."

"Huh?" Sam slumped as he faced control buttons, levers and lit icons for apps with none showing something like a leaf tumbling in the wind, which as far as he was concerned, was the universal symbol for a situation where the pilot soars to save the day, only to crash-land and get a beam rammed through the chest.

One good thing—the altimeter showed they were two hundred thousand feet up and traveling horizontally, not vertically and ascending to leave the atmosphere.

"The grooves suggest the bottom of the pod can be opened, like aircrafts from the world wars that dropped bombs," Kurt said, his voice tone flat.

*Dispose of bodies over the oceans?* "Holy crap. But that's a lot for fish to eat." Sam flinched. *Way to go, numbnuts.* The guy's murdered bride was scheduled to be dumped into the sea? "Er…sorry. I can't imagine what you're feeling right now. It's just…I wouldn't think they'd take the chance remains would wash ashore."

Kurt snorted. "Good point and here's another fact. Speaking as an amateur geologist, there's five hundred active volcanoes on Earth."

"Christ."

"No. I think he's long fled this planet."

Sam straightened his shoulders. "Okay. It also means if I don't figure out how to take control from autopilot soon, we'll probably fly over the closest volcano to our starting point, hover and drop, and proceed to land in a secret underground or underwater base on some spot right here on good ol' godforsaken Earth." He jerked his hands from the wheel, and punched his correct code into his corrupted wrist phone. "Kurt, watch for seagulls and rainclouds while I stir up a few billion souls to help us select a place to land before a heat-seeking missile does the job. They'll notice the second we go off course."

"Who you gonna message with that kind of clout? You know Jack Bauer isn't real, right?"

Jack Bauer was a character in an ancient TV series. His name had become synonymous with an unrealistic hero who could defeat the bad guys before a day ended. Sam chuckled. "Who needs twenty-four hours? The Net's being flooded as we speak. My name is Dexter."

Kurt's eyes went wide. "Sam Dexter? *In the Loop* is your blog?"

"Guilty."

"Fantastic." Kurt cracked a smile. "If they don't have time to utilize those missiles, maybe we're not all dead. You understand the audio controls? We have to get a hold of someone who isn't connected with the Love Center to talk us down."

# Chapter Ten

The shuttle's nose angled wrong, automated control for the damn landing wheels nowhere to be found, Sam hit the runway like he'd never flown any type of aircraft before.

Kurt saved him from more than ribs cracking after he shot forward and sharp knobs tried to impale him.

Thousands had clustered at the airport, closed to all traffic but crashing shuttles. Men and women cheered, screaming questions and encouragement while medics descended on them. Clearly the blog post had gone viral. He'd have to get online and post a follow-up to his status before the area became so overrun by anxious fans that authorities broke out the teargas — or worse.

Over a grueling hour later, Sam sprawled on a hospital bed that was raised so he could partially sit with heart pounding and head aching, his brain on overdrive with worry.

Upon being wheeled into this place, they'd stripped him, but no one had dared to confiscate his wrist phone. Then a medic hadn't hesitated to place a lap-com in front of him, so he didn't have to peck away at wrist phone keys.

He'd encouraged his online fans to do what they could to help authorities ensure the safety of those on the other shuttles, and give him time to situate himself before he shared a detailed summary of what he knew. He posted his hopes that world leaders would quiet civil unrest by going public with constant newsfeeds on what they were doing to ferret out and arrest the monsters in their midst.

Fingers shaking, he'd added his belief that stopping him from feeding the world the truths he knew — dedicated followers debating every word to know for sure they were his — would result in potential mass hysteria. People would not only protect him, the whistleblower, but in the confusion, honest leaders could be accused and discriminated against, as well as those proven to be guilty of crimes against humanity on a scale not seen since twentieth century concentration camps. He ended his post with the promise of consistent updates on his wellbeing, including when he'd switch to video feeds.

Now he couldn't take the stress any longer. Time to concentrate on his own needs. He set aside the lap-com and took the bellowing up a notch because the dickheads in this medical center had yet to bring a woman to the secured room they'd confined him to — a woman he very much needed to see before he could think about escaping, burrowing underground somewhere he'd dare to close his eyes.

Authorities and fans wanted so many pieces of him, Sam felt like he was on the verge of exploding and giving them just that. Over thirty-six hours without sleep, he'd soon not be able to manage more than grunts, monosyllables and smashing his fist into someone's face.

He glowered at the two male medics hovering nearby. "Return my clothes and unlock the door. I'll find my wife" —*how I wish that was true*—"myself. Please."

They'd tucked him away in this solitary room and guarded the exit. The medical center personnel wouldn't stop sneaking pictures of him wearing nothing but a hospital wrap, open to his navel and held together in the back by flimsy ties. Everyone gawked as if he was hot stuff, like a rock star, movie star or political comedian, when in reality he was nothing but a selfish guy who feared to get word out concerning the real hero—not until she was safe from being fawned over by anyone other than himself. Except, in his case, he prayed it'd be much more than a mere fawning. In fact, he was so nerved up, he should drag himself into the bathroom and relieve the pressure. Take the edge off so he didn't jump the moment bozos cooperated and she walked into this room.

One of the medics cleared his throat. "I'll ask again, Mister Dexter." He tapped at his wrist phone and a moment later raised his gaze to Sam. "I...um...told my superior you'd be more cooperative concerning the debriefing after you and Miss Jensen were reunited."

*Her last name's Jensen?* The entire world knew more about Jenna than he did. These guys also knew his last name and hers wasn't Bond, and that the marriage was as legit as the shuttles had been. He sighed. Hard to feel sorry for himself. At least they'd survived when so many hadn't. But damn it, what if Jenna wasn't all right? Harmed? Even tortured? Disappeared into the system and held hostage until he refuted everything?

"And?" he snapped.

"Any minute now."

Sam leaned back into the pillows, his throat suddenly dry.

The second medic stood in place, shifting uneasily while the other medic approached. "Sorry, sir, but you know they won't leave you with Miss Jensen for too long. Too many questions." He leaned to straighten the sheet over Sam's legs and mouthed, *"Bugs."*

Sam sighed. He had expected such. Deadly power mongers with ties to the LC must want a recording of every breath and every word from the peon who defied them with nothing but a whim and a platform for the common man.

He deepened his scowl and braced to rasp the truth to his new friend. "It's clear you guys know I'm not really a newlywed. But I'll remain a pain in the ass if I don't have a chance—in private—to see what's happening with me and the real hero, who's an innocent—big stress on the word innocent. Maybe she wants to fake divorce a high-profile guy who almost got her killed. Not really fair to do that online, without the chance for a kiss goodbye, is it?"

"As soon as she's here, we'll wait in the corridor. I hope you can work things out." The guy mouthed, *"Body scan,"* straightened and stepped back.

Neurons began clicking. *Of course. And this man, maybe both medics, would clearly help.* The irritation strangling his gut lessened. He needed to give authorities reason to move him to an unsecured location. A scan didn't make sense. The imaging room had to be wired with all types of audio and video surveillance. Maybe the medic's blank expression meant if Sam got the ball rolling, he'd take it from there. Help him seize a stolen moment of unwatched and unheard freedom, and the guy needed some sort of pretense to get him out of this room to make it happen.

Sam nodded. "Thank you."

The medic reclaimed the steps for the bed. He fussed with the upper strap on Sam's chest. "It's not a problem. We're monitoring you closely. Just let us know if you need anything at all." The guy patted his leg and retreated.

*Hm.* Must be wireless sensors inside the two thin plastic bands they'd tied around his chest to support damaged ribs. At least he'd caught a break with the pair in the room with him. He could use all the help he could get, and not just to arrange a chance to speak in private with Jenna. He also had to slip past riled fans ready to riot if they saw him but wince in pain, as well as authorities prepared to maintain order no matter the cost to the environment or to enthusiastic admirers of *In the Loop.*

He smiled at the dark-haired medic. "What was your name?"

"Thomas…"

The door com buzzed and Sam's heartbeat lurched as the door pushed open. A man, dressed in a dark suit, ushered in a wonderful sight. Jenna looked at him with clarity and no signs of ill treatment. Hair tangled, face bruised, rings of exhaustion beneath those wide, questioning eyes, and he ached to wrap his arms around her. His damn cock went stiff, throbbing to skip the holding and proceed directly to the having. He swallowed hard. "Leave us alone." He didn't take his gaze from her.

As the three men exited, the medic…Thomas paused. "We'll be right outside."

"Yep." The door closed.

"Hi, sweetheart. You okay?" He didn't pause. "Pardon, my head's all fogged. Almost like the first time I met you." *You know, when we were afraid every word was being recorded.* "Must be the painkillers, but I forget the strangest things. Your name's really Jenna?"

"It is." The mouth of the most beautiful and most intelligent woman in the universe opened in a soft circle of dismay. "You've hurt ribs?"

"No." He flung out an arm, smothering his groan. "Come here."

"Are you lying?"

He arched his brows. "I'm Superman. I'm fine."

"You need to rest."

"Don't make me get up." He patted the bed beside him. "Best spot on Earth for a honeymoon." His heart did flips as color rose in her cheeks and she closed in.

"Doesn't your chest hurt?" Jenna carefully sat next to him.

He hit the button to recline and his arm couldn't go around her fast enough. "Not since the moment you entered this room," he lied. "I've made a full recovery." *Ohgodohgod, another second and I'll have her beneath me.* He leaned for her ear and whispered, "The lead's mine. Play along."

Like rolling into heaven, Sam pushed her down. Without care that her eyes went as wide as the moon, he climbed on top. His body, ribs were numb to pretty much anything but doing as his cock begged, which was to lower himself to pin her. Even his mind got in on the action, rationalizing who cared they were being filmed — *give them a porno tape to knock their jealous socks off* — as he supported his weight with his elbows. He pushed a harsh yelp out, instead of begging her — *say yes, say yes, say yes.* His groan of frustration flung him from the clouds into hot and bothered hell and hopefully sounded to the listeners as if he were dying.

"What's wrong?" Jenna gasped. Her shiny dark hair splashed across the pillow, blood draining from her cheeks as her eyes widened with worry. She grasped his arms to push at him.

He winked at her and refused to budge. He barked another cry of exaggerated hurt as his throbbing dick grew, and groaned, pressing into her stomach. God, she felt so good, smashed beneath him. He eased up a touch so she could breathe and let out a final pain-wracked gulp. "I-I think my ribs just cracked." Propped on his elbow, he thrust his hand to rub at his skull. "But my head hurts, more than anything."

The door shot open. "Dexter, what is it?" Thomas grasped his shoulder, forcing him to shift off a flustered Jenna. He drew his knee up, frantically willing his cock to go down.

"Wrong? Not a damn…arrggg." He collapsed flat and moaned. "Head hurts. Something *is* wrong."

The suit shoved Thomas aside. "Get off the bed, lady. You do something to him?"

Sam seized Jenna's arm and glared at the suit. "Back off." He grunted as if he was being gutted by a wild boar and thank Christ, his lovely girl looked confused as all hell, but she kept her mouth closed.

"It's not her," Thomas said. "TBM has bad side effects."

"TBM?" asked the guy with government agent written all over him.

"Temazoan-Benzo-Morphine." Thomas followed the second medic running around the bed.

"And that means?" snapped the agent.

Thomas helped the other medic turn the bed and wheel it for the door. "An illegal and complex time-release drug cocktail concentrated into a soluble capsule. It was the reason Mr. Dexter survived the gas in those pods and was able to escape the one he was in. He needs a full head CT — stat."

Sam maintained his hold on Jenna. "Fine. But my…Ms. Jensen comes with me."

"That's not a good idea," said the agent.

"Try to separate us," Sam moaned, "and I'll make sure the brain matter containing all the future blog posts that fans — over nine billion and climbing — won't have chance to read, splatters on you when my skull splits."

Five minutes later, they shoved the bed holding Sam and Jenna out from the elevator and down the hallway toward radiology.

"We might as well prep you on the way." Thomas pushed the gurney with one hand and reached for Sam's chest, while the other medic leaned over Jenna's shoulder. She hadn't said a word, and held onto him even tighter as the men unclipped the double brace around his chest. His suspicion that the agent stalked behind them was confirmed when the guy spoke up.

"Why are you taking those off?"

Sam eased his body forward. Thomas pulled the top band out from under and the other guy took the bottom one. "These bands aren't solid plastic," Thomas told the agent. "Metal doesn't work well in imaging." He picked up the pace and addressed Sam. "Keep still. Might start to hurt, but when you're out of the machine, we'll strap you up again."

The corridor widened and split toward the imaging reception area. The woman at the counter looked up as they stopped in the corridor, and Thomas hurried forward. They spoke briefly and he stepped back.

"Ten minutes?" the other medic asked.

"More like a half hour. A man just went in. He's critical." Thomas grasped the bed. "We shouldn't block the hall." He wheeled the bed toward a door opposite them.

"That's unacceptable," the agent called out. "Get Dexter in there now."

A small medical center, there must be only one CT machine. Sam doubted Thomas would lie. He'd know the agent would check to see if there was a patient in there, and no way would Sam risk someone's wellbeing for a fake headache. He squeezed Jenna's hand. "I'll wait. Don't want another potential death to be blamed on the government, do we?"

"He's stable, sir," Thomas told the agent. "We'll proceed if that changes."

The second medic opened the door, and Thomas pushed them into a stockroom with barely enough space for the gurney.

Sam settled back and closed his eyes. "This is good. Really. Maybe all I need is a half hour of quiet. Leave. Close the door."

"Er... We'll be close, within calling distance." Thomas paused. "Speak up if his pain gets worse."

"I will," Jenna whispered. "Thanks."

The moment he heard the door close, Sam snapped his eyes open, released Jenna's hand and sat up. Open shelves of toiletries and cleaning supplies on either side. No large cupboards, closets or shadowy forms. He looked in all directions, including the ceiling, and bent to peer beneath the bed.

*Alone at last.* A lazy grin spread across his face as he slumped on his side, turning to the woman beside him. If only they had longer. The things he'd do to her. He lost the smile and muttered, "We can talk softly now. Gotta get out of here, sweetheart. I should have a ride coming. I think at least one medic, that Thomas, will help me dodge security."

Huge brown eyes stared at him. "Where to?"

"Underground. Between the sociopaths behind the LC and fans ready to eat me up, I'm a sitting duck if I don't go off the grid. Kurt and I talked before landing. He said he'd find a Jeep, stock it and somehow get word to me where he'll wait. Said if he couldn't, he'd enlist help to storm this place and clear a path."

Sam sincerely hoped it wouldn't come to that. Kurt fought depression as well as intense anger. A big guy, he'd killed the goon on the shuttle without hesitation. He'd not think twice about red dots on his chest or snapping more thick necks if he was denied access to Sam.

Jenna stiffened, her body shying away from him. "How soon?"

*Hey, I only beat up one guy. A pervert with a pilot license. Doesn't she want to be with me, a criminal going on the run?*
"We decided four hours maximum, meaning less than an hour from now."

"Oh. Sam?" Jenna swallowed as if her throat was as dry as his. "I didn't get a chance to tell you about theories I ran across in chat rooms. When you've a chance, you should check their accuracy. There was strong insistence that facts correlating with the pollution index, and based on carbon dioxide ratios in dense sections, place the world's population closer to ten or eleven billion, not eighteen."

*That's why I only have nine billion followers?* His heart stopped beating as the less narcissistic implications sank in. "Those bastards killed eight billion newlyweds? Christ. I thought these were the first shuttle launches." *So much for not being vindictive. Bloody rampage, here I come.*

Jenna snorted. "No, you idiot, we are...*were* the first group."

He stared at her.

"Governments lied about planet population," she said. "A thousand shuttles, fifty pods in each, luckily timed to depart within minutes of each other around the world at Eastern Standard Time on the North America continent, meant schedules were hours apart. The math sucks but thanks to some hero, eight hundred and five fake rockets never took off."

He relaxed, muscles going slack. "I could get used to that."

She leaned over him, ducking her head to hide the hurt filling her eyes. "You can't be serious. Used to another cover-up so the powers-that-be can own pockets of expensive land?"

"Nope. Being called an idiot." *Yippee ki-yay. My insecure, pretend bride* does *want me.* He put his thumb under her chin and raised her gaze to his. "Even if I could handle the chemistry involved in population grids, exposing conspiracies requires finesse. Very risky for a couple of guys like me and Kurt."

"Are you asking me...?"

"I am." He reached his palm to her chest, over her heart. "What type of hero would let you—a target for sexual predators in backward bars—out of his sight? And speaking of idiots... That had to be the stupidest means to get someone's attention ever. I saw a survivor staring at you before medics dragged me away. His eyes were reddened, like he'd been recently hit with pepper spray."

His hand on her chest felt the jump in Jenna's heartbeat and it angered him immensely. "Damn him, beating the fuckin' odds. He's the guy you texted to meet you in that bar before me. Did he hurt you?" *I'll kill him.*

She blinked, flinching from his glare. "No."

"Look at me. Did he force you?"

She raised and held her gaze on his. "I can take care of myself. Forget him."

Not likely. The guy had at least tried. Probably did more than try before she'd outsmarted the prick. Not right an asshole survived while Kurt's wife hadn't. Should he yell at the unfair universe until Jenna promised to at least press charges?

Or should he forestall the righteous indignation until later? Seize this carefully arranged moment and keep blood galloping south instead of being diverted to harden his fingers into fists. He sucked in a deep breath. *Damn. Hurt.* His ribs ached…and suddenly they didn't.

Insane that he hadn't noticed before, but whiffs of cinnamon, almond and something subtly arousing had his cock in a tizzy, rearing up to take center stage. The woman beside him—in a bed for the first time with him—smelled wildly invigorating. Whatever vigilante crap he'd been thinking took a sharp right turn toward the land of Not-now-imbecile. Later, he'd contemplate how easily thoughts of violence came to him, a hardened brute who'd smacked a bottle against a man's head. The operative word, in these dwindling stolen minutes, being hard. He unclenched his fists and soothed his fingers along Jenna's arm as he concentrated on her whisper.

"You're the most famous man alive. The Love Center is on its knees denying everything, but unable to hide all those shuttles primed with poisoned gas. Governments will fall. The United World—sold on everyone living on peaceful planets, striving for utopia—is grieving and furious." Color rose in Jenna's cheeks and she faltered. "I need to apologize. I'm the one who may have gotten to you in this mess."

"In bed with you is a mess?" *Tick tock.* He slipped his hand to her lower back. *Hot to trot.* "I beg to differ." *Cock wants out. Now!*

Her blush deepened. "I've...um followed you for years. You know me. I comment as JJ. My name is Jenna Jensen."

His hand stilled. Every inch of him began cheering and praying his ears heard right. *Oh dear God, could life get more perfect?* "You're JJ? Fantastic. I think I love you." He knew he did. "I lived for your replies. Tagged them so comments go directly to my inbox. Been the highlight after posting for a decade, reading your thoughts and a few others' while ignoring the fluff. You know, want to send pictures, marry, have my children, skin me alive and so on."

She remained silent, her lower lip trembling.

"What's wrong?" *Balls.* If she was married or involved, worried because he'd said the love word, he'd...kidnap her and grovel to her and the husband. Beg her to let him be something to her, even do a sharing type thing if she'd just let him be a part of their lives.

He swallowed hard. "What is it?"

"I suggested you look into the LC, remember?"

"Yes. And billions will thank you. That, I promise." He stared at her. "Go on... Tell me."

"I... In the bar. I pushed myself on you and lied to you."

*She is married. Fuck-fuck-fuck.* "Lied?"

"I'm not an escort, hooker, whatever."

His laugh burst out, a bark of relief, and pain throbbed through him at the sudden movement. "I know that."

"I'm a fan, yes." She sighed and her low voice grew even quieter. "But not some groupie. Don't worry. If there's a problem—which I doubt—I won't even tell you if I decide on an abortion or not."

His brain came to a screeching halt.

"You don't have to make it seem like I'm anything to you," she continued. "You don't know me. I…"

*I could be a father. I could have and hold the mother of my child for longer than a pair bonded by a near-death experience that drift apart once the dust settles. I think she could love me. Me. A dad. Me. A dad. Me…*

"Are you listening?"

"Always." He tightened his arm around her. "It was your call. I'd have stopped. You said yes. But I didn't grab a condom from the dispenser hanging on the wall and I have rights, too. I'm no longer asking. You're coming with me if I have to carry you kicking and screaming. We'll debate insecurities and parental rights while dodging bullets because if you think the Love Center's on its knees, you're more naïve than any sweetheart I can ever hope to kiss again. Understand?"

"No. I stopped listening past me caveman who does as he wants."

He chuckled.

She peeked at him beneath thick lashes. "Ever hope to kiss again?"

He didn't hesitate. Kept the kiss short and sweet, the clock ticking. He pulled back and licked his lips, the taste of her one he never wanted to miss again. *Mine. All mine. I won't lose her and God, how I want her.* He smirked. "It's good luck to seal an agreement to go on the lam with more than a kiss."

"Is that so?" she drawled. "Broken ribs and minutes before that agent bursts in here?"

*Yippee time again.* No argument that she hadn't said she'd go with him. "They're not broken. The clock in my head says we have fifteen minutes and memory tells me you're a firecracker." He loved the blood rising in her cheeks. "A honeymoon requires slow savoring and repeats. I give my word, and if you really are JJ, you know what the integrity of words means to me. Jenna, sweetheart. We'll have a honeymoon for a lifetime if you promise to obey—make that love—me, through violence and healing and running from fans and paparazzi and angry power mongers and a good chance I'll get you killed. Say yes."

"Yes," she whispered. "For now. Okay?"

*Gentle, you fool.* He slapped her butt. "No. More. I want you and a maybe-baby and a dog and a garden and a tea cozy and a picket—"

His heart sank as she tugged free of him and rolled off the bed.

"Okay, fine. I'll take anything, anyway you want it."

She hit the button, shifting the back half of the bed up as she adjusted the pillow behind him. "You won't be going anywhere if you puncture a lung. Behave."

He shook his head and patted his stomach. "Sit on top of me and we'll give the guys a show when they open that door."

She scowled.

*Not wasting another second.* He lurched to grab her. Jaw clenched against the complaining bones in his chest, he lifted her to straddle him and homed in. To his joy, she didn't hesitate and her mouth responded to his with aggression. He took her backward with him to rest against the pillow, while she eased her arm around his neck and deepened the kiss.

Their tongues dueled with a frantic need to please each other, and his skin began to hum as he caressed her most seductive rump to work at her skirt. Without breaking the kiss, she pushed up on her knees, making it easy for him to find the side zipper. Her tongue gave way to his, and she gasped and moaned into his mouth as his cock tented the flimsy hospital gown and his fingers fumbled. He felt like his ribs melted into pliable plastic, all energy concentrated in his throbbing dick.

She groaned, easing her head back and breaking the kiss. He gulped a shallow breath while she mumbled, "This isn't a good idea. There's no time, and I have to be hurting you."

"You are." He grunted. "Oh God—it's agony. Get out of that blouse. Please. We have to seize…" He lost his train of thought as she shifted to her knees, and his hands sprang to attack the top button. *Fast, faster— whoa.* He froze on the third button down. There was something pink, silky and girlie beneath the pleated top, not the simple bra he'd expected. Lingerie in case evil bastards hadn't existed and that shuttle had taken them to the moon?

A mental slap upside his head helped him focus and he came to a sweet and horrific conclusion. She'd hoped to be swept off her feet, carried to the bed by a devoted groom who had all the time in the world?

But assholes would drag him to an imaging machine any moment.

*So what? Carpe diem. Do her. In-out-repeat. Hurry.*

His hands remembered how to work as he stared. Oh Christ, some sort of classy, intricate netting made of silk threads hugged her chest. A deep bob of his Adam's apple and he wouldn't stop himself for taking on button number four and five, even if she changed her mind…Well, he would, then die of disappointment. A rising tsunami of testosterone swamped him, wiping out exhaustion and any care of bruised bones other than one. His wood and pecker combined, tapping against the soft dip of her stomach, begging to be aimed lower and — *oops* — he popped the last three buttons. They shot out and hit the floor with pings.

Jenna's breath hitched, and she shrugged off the blouse. He leaned back, his jaw slack as he absorbed the sight of breasts supported by the sexiest strips of material he'd ever seen. Some sort of pink, darker pink and black camisole that left pebbled nipples exposed and begging for his mouth.

"Oh God," he croaked. "You're so beautiful." More than beautiful. Sugar and spice, the hottest thing a man could ever hope for on the best night of his life. God, it hurt, how much he wished they had a real honeymoon ahead of them. *I can't do another wham-bam like in the bar, can I?*

He felt the heat swamp his neck. All he cared about was getting off? Not making solid plans to ensure her safety, but treat the woman of the hour like a common bathroom fuck. A woman he known for a mere few days in real space, but she'd commented on his blog for a decade. Not being a total dimwit, he could read between the lines of what she'd written over the years. Highly empathic and intelligent, she was also a dippy romantic — worse that he was.

He forced his shaking hands from her and dropped his arms to bang against the bed. "I'm sorry. You deserve a man without a ticking countdown to being dragged away by either friend or foe. You smell fantastic, look so pretty and sexy I can barely say this." He swallowed hard and flicked his hand toward the shelves of cleaning fluids. "Quickie in a bathroom stall or a utility closet, what type of jerk does that to a sweetheart like you?"

# Chapter Eleven

Her skirt unzipped on one side, blouse off and breasts exposed through the risqué camisole, Jenna sat on top of Sam's legs. He stared at her face not her body, the lust in his eyes turned to doubt—emotion his erection didn't share.

Bunched at his knees, the hospital gown made a lovely pyramid at his crotch, moist where the tip of his cock leaked, and she found herself resenting a single drop being wasted on the fabric. His obvious interest showed he couldn't care less he'd not had any sleep for ages, survived poisoning and a crash—and had a battered chest no longer supported by braces.

If none of that gave him pause to release the sheet at his sides and rip the priciest bit of clothing she'd ever brought off her, what was his problem? He couldn't give her another five wonderful minutes of banging before some guy rescued him from the groupies surrounding this medical center? Her heartbeat faltered. Some of them, pretty young women she'd caught a glimpse of before being shut in a waiting area, wore T-shirts with *We Love SD* written across the front, and on the back — *In TheLoop Any Loophole, Front or Back.*

She thrust out her lower lip. "You're going to hold onto the sheet with both hands until they come to either X-ray your brain or sneak you — us — out of here?"

"Us," he growled. "Us."

"But nothing happens in the short time we have left."

His face fell. "I told you. You expected — deserve — so much more."

Because she'd dressed to seduce, he thought her high-maintenance? Like the bride he was supposed to be with, a woman who'd never settle for fast and furious in a bathroom or utility closet?

That familiar feeling, the python named Insecurity, slithered to squeeze the air from her lungs. Maybe it wasn't that simple. Could be he'd put the brakes on because he worried they really could conceive a child. Realized every woman and gay on this planet wanted to sit where she was and that the door might open the moment things got hotter than a couple of kisses. Cameras would flash, and the world would know he was with a short, skinny nerd.

She should give up the Cinderella dream... *No. Please no.* Lust jolted through her veins, strangling the python and leaving her empty and yearning. She wished she dared to place her tongue where his was as he licked his lips, leaving her bracing for the shivers to race up her spine as he spoke in that sexy, gravelly voice.

"After all this settles down and we find a place to become anonymous, we can at least do the flowers and dinner thing first, right?"

Wrong. Poor man didn't have a good memory. Only a total loser wouldn't take advantage of that. She'd already showed him once that she knew how low to aim, how gently to squeeze. She shot her hand out and grasped that tent. His mouth fell softly open and he made no move to stop her. Instead, his rough pant told her he hung on by a thread.

She stared into his eyes, bright green going darker and darker with heat, and clutched her fingers around the base of wondrously hard wood, the long thick cock poised and quivering in front of her as she drew the thin cotton fabric up. *Stroke-stroke-sob, he's so lovely.* The veins in his cock throbbed beneath her fingers and he moaned, fisting the sheet with both hands.

"There's...You sure about this?"

She frowned. "Yes. No. But if you ever want to use this again," a downward sweep of her hand on his cock and his groan grew desperate, "tell me the truth."

"Truth?" he grunted.

"Why'd you stop? Maybe you're worried about birth control?" She gulped, forcing herself to continue. "Or that woman at the bar?"

His eyes narrowed. "What woman?"

She bent, and blew over the head of his cock trying to burst through the sheet. "Answer the question or in one minute, my fake husband, you'll spill into this hospital gown." *You can't know how self-doubting I really am, can you?*

He laughed. "You've a lot to learn about me, my fake wife. More like ten seconds." He seized her upper arms and reared up to halt his lips inches from hers. "I forgot the question, but I'll tell you the truth as often as you need to hear it."

*Oh God, he does know and he really does want* me? *Please, say it again.*

He yanked the un-zippered side of her skirt round. "I want you. Only you." He rammed his hand up beneath it. "I want a maybe-child." Her lungs locked as he wrenched her panties aside. "I want...Nah. Who cares

143

about picket fences or...a thong, too? Dear God." He cupped her sex and in a smooth flow of muscles flipped her onto her back. "I want to look at every bit of you. You feel so soft, pretty—"

"Move. Now." She grasped his hipbones. He lifted upward and she helped him pull up the gown to free his cock.

"Ohh..." No hesitation, his bare cockhead butted against the thin slit of the thong and they both groaned. He felt wonderful, ready to power down into her, her muscles anxious to grasp and keep him inside her, only...

*Hello? Stupid girl?*

Damn it, her brain wanted a word. *Fine,* she grudgingly thought. Point one tenth of a second to rationalize. *Hurry,* she snapped to herself. Positioning was set, the most expert cock in the world rubbing her, widening her, making sure she was more than ready for a deep, driving manic burst of power drilling...*oh God, whaaat is the deal?*

*It's simple. You're gonna lose him. Remember him? The guy you swore to rescue? Think this is over? Idiot. There's no time. Not with this guy who'll rally for a proper pounding. Make this right and fast. It'll... He'll be delicious.*

"Sam...Sam, wait." She gave herself a mental slap. It was crazy for her to act as if everything was fine when it really wasn't. Not with governments in turmoil, the most powerful corporation on Earth pissed and vengeful and the posse waiting outside the door.

"What...?" Sam gasped. Frozen in place, he blinked as he stared at her, his arms trembling with the effort to hold back. "You all right?"

She smiled. "Yes. Get off. Please."

Guilt flashed in his eyes. He rolled to his side and jerked to avoid falling off the bed as he mumbled, "I'm a pig. Too fast. No fun for you. I'm sorry."

"Don't be." She hopped off the bed, straightened her skirt and zipped up.

He started to work the hospital gown down his chest, cover himself, and she muttered, "Leave it. Hang on a second."

"Huh?" His long lashes lowered, his face downcast, as she grabbed her blouse.

"It's me that's selfish." She slipped the blouse on, no time to mess with buttons. "Being insecure and all, I didn't want to take the lead—and that's a big…" Oh yeah, was he ever. Her thighs clenched. She didn't need him inside her. She was about to rocket, just looking at him.

"Big?" he croaked.

"Mistake. Trusting you, I mean." *Get with it, girl. Yum, yum, yum.* She slapped her palm on his bare stomach and his beautiful eyes widened. "Not that I don't love… Well, I imagine I'd love vanilla sex with you on top, but I shouldn't be on my back. You should." She licked her lips, her attention glued on his yearning cock.

*Never gonna fit.*

*Shut up. I'll take what I can. In this moment, he's mine. Every thick inch.* "Well, you're on your back now and I need to think."

The trail of dark hairs narrowed beneath the gown bunched on his upper chest, forming a tantalizing path south. His skin quivered beneath her hand. "Think? About what? The fact I'm about to embarrass myself into your face?"

"Oh no." She giggled. "I'm way too hungry to let that happen." She lowered parted lips and blew on his glistening cock with its pre-cum dripping. "Just keep your hands to yourself and be as quiet as you can."

"No touching you?"

"That's the deal," she whispered. Another hot breath from her, her tongue poked out between her lips, and whatever undecipherable thing he'd started to mutter turned into strangled sounds as he raised his hips. "Oh…goood…God-d-d…"

"Shh." She pushed down on his abdomen. Her other hand hurried to grasp the base of his cock. "Relax… Well, not this part." She licked the tip, round and round, sucked and lapped — *delicious* — and slid her mouth down to take him as deep as she could. Not an expert, but the hot light in his eyes, the way his body trembled and how he tried not to choke her only made her want to swallow — *oh wow* — she felt him hit the back of her throat. He gulped and she sucked harder as she drew her mouth and hand up together, popping the head of his cock out. She licked and nibbled back down his length, mumbling, "I think…best when I'm…doing something active, you know what I mean?"

"Oh. And hell no, I can't think… Christ, that…feels great. Please don't stop… Think about what?"

She halted. "Your plan to just waltz out of here and head for the hills sucks. After I'm done sucking, it's your turn to follow my lead. Okay?"

Hmm, so good, but no answer from the guy with his mouth gaping. Just because she nibbled and lapped the length of him, he'd lost cognitive function? Nothing but a harsh rasp from his throat as her own became chock-full of lip-smacking cock. She released one of her hands from his base and reached for his balls. Rubbing them gently together like a pair of heavy pebbles, she ran her thumb over the tightening sac.

He shuddered, groaning quietly and grabbing at the sheet from both sides. She raised her head, forcing herself to let the treat plop from her mouth, her fingers back to tracing the hard line between his balls. "Hey, you haven't answered me yet."

"Oh." He grunted. "Sorry. Of course I won't come—"

"What?" she snapped. "You'd better come in my mouth. Every drop."

"Sure. Hell, yes." He swallowed hard. "Could you continue...er...right now?"

"Not that, you idiot. You'll trust me when the door opens?"

His Adam's apple bobbed again and he closed his eyes. "I'll follow you anywhere. And I'm not just saying that because I'm frantic for any sort of ending."

She parted her lips, took and took and took not even close to every inch, bobbing up and down. His eyelids fluttered. He stiffened, his balls so hard and drawn beneath her fingers she worried he'd explode. He did, jerking and partially pulling out so she didn't drown. Warm cum filled her mouth, squirt after squirt, and leaked between her lips.

He collapsed, eyes still closed, and his lips curved into a soft smile as she licked him clean. She got every salty drop that'd escaped her mouth, tucked his satiated cock down and caressed up his chest for the hospital gown.

Those deep green eyes opened. He partially sat up and helped her cover him. "Sweetheart, what exactly did I promise, other than to spend the rest of my life not letting you out of my sight?" He tilted his head, watching her intently as she stepped back, fastening what buttons were left on her blouse.

She shrugged. "Not to argue. No making a big deal out of anything other than thinking of those ribs and how it feels knowing you're the man that everyone wants to thank." *And the hordes of women waiting to take you away from me, who wish to thank you with much more than smile.*

"But I'm not the hero."

She sighed and faced the door. *You are to me, and I wish I could keep you.* "Thomas?" she called out. "Come on in, you guys. He's all better now and ready to walk out the front entrance."

The door opened.

A tall, bronze-skinned woman—yet another damn suit—stood in the doorway. "We'll see about that." Her gaze held the dank, cold expression Jenna imagined a dead fish would wear. The woman entered alone, closed the door and looked to the bed. "Mister Dexter. Now that you've been pleasured, is anything wrong other than bruised ribs? Is this headache real?"

Heat rushed to Jenna's face, and her knees wobbled as the woman took in her tousled hair and overly red lips while a harsh snort came from Sam.

"Cameras—or did you crack the door open?" he snapped. "Couldn't let us have a brief window of privacy?" His legs twisted. He sat and his feet hit the floor.

"Hmm." The woman pursed her lips. "Answering a question with another. Standard procedure when one expects not to be forthright, is it not?"

Sam's scowl deepened. "No doubt. Here's some truth. You're all assholes. I want my clothes. We *are* leaving. Now." He started to push to his feet, lines of exhaustion etched beneath his eyes.

"Wait a moment," Jenna said. "Sit still." She turned to the intimidating woman. "He's just shattered. Needs a solid sleep."

The woman nodded. "The head pain?"

"A means so we could discuss how best to get out of here," Jenna said. "Who are you?"

"Chief Admiral of the United Governments, Doctor of Justice, Assistant CEO for World Forces and General Prosecutor for the North America Continent."

Jenna crossed her arms over her chest, unable to hide the bright pink lace peeking from the lower part of her blouse. "You don't have a name?"

"Either sir or ma'am will do."

A large hand eased down to clasp her shoulder and she wilted. Sam stood beside her in the rumpled green gown reaching to his knees, looking much more dignified than her. Was this admiral about to have him escorted to an interrogation room in some secretive building, where he'd be wide open for corrupt officials to take a shot at? That's how it'd play out for a guy who risked everything to expose plans to eliminate fertile humans that'd blossomed in the midst of so many authorities it was beyond pathetic?

"Skip the posturing, lady." Sam squeezed Jenna's shoulder. "I concede your gun's bigger than ours."

A flicker of annoyance went through the dark eyes of the woman blocking the door. "Olivia Keltz. Is what Miss Jensen said true, Mister Dexter? You lied concerning your health in order to plot how best to avoid further questioning on the role you played in this alleged conspiracy?"

"Yes." Sam lowered his arm. He tugged at Jenna until she took his hand. "Any video shows up on the Net, I'll make sure every person on this planet knows who the alleged voyeur is. Where are my clothes?"

Keltz didn't blink. Not an eyelash flickered. "There is no video. My aide looked in and informed me and me alone. I made the executive decision to grant you a few more minutes. Moving on. Clothes belonging to you are not in this facility. The pilot uniform is evidence and clearly was stolen."

"You're here on behalf of the LC?" Sam bit out the question.

"The LC has been shut down pending investigation." Keltz reached into the top pocket of her suit and flashed a badge. "I told you my credentials. As lead prosecutor for this area of the world, I take personal charge of high-profile suspects fit to be transported to a holding cell or more secure medical facilities." The woman angled her arm to tap at her wrist phone. "And a holding area it shall be."

Jenna gasped. "You're arresting him? For what?"

"Assault and battery. Theft of identity and property to include a handgun that was found with incriminating fingerprints tossed beneath the ramp of the shuttle he severely damaged. Possession of a weapon of mass destruction found at his apartment. Perchance murder. It's not clear who broke the neck of an LC employee found on the shuttle."

Her heart pounding erratically, Jenna's jaw dropped.

"Is that all?" Sam drawled in a dry voice.

"No. Brace yourself, young man." The brief twitch of Keltz's lips, a pathetic attempt at a smile, frightened Jenna more than anything else about her. "There's a situation that has developed that some may deem worse than the mandatory death sentences for crimes already listed." Keltz snorted. "Lose the scowl, son. If not for me, a different pair of eyes would have seen what I hear is a decently sized item. Although, in retrospect I'm sure that ship has sailed more than once."

"What the f-f— What are you talking about?" Sam sputtered.

Keltz dipped her head. "Your wife, Mister Dexter, is lawyered up and pacing in the lobby of this building. Insists she be allowed to oversee your wellbeing and pending legal problems."

"My wife?" Sam dropped Jenna's hand. Blood drained from his face. "Balls. Seriously?"

Keltz gestured at the bed. "Sit down. Answer me honestly and I can make all this — legit and non-legit wife included — go away."

An imaginary judge's gavel punched Jenna in the gut. Of course. Sam had signed a marriage contract with the blonde she'd seen at the bar. Naturally, Miss…Mrs. Perfect wouldn't contest it. After all, *her* husband was currently the hottest guy on this planet. While Jenna, Miss Forger, stood there with the guilty taste of cum in her throat, the most notorious fake-hooker.

Jenna remained rooted to the floor as Keltz strode forward. Sam was no longer white. He'd gone a weary shade of gray. Keltz grasped his elbow and pushed him backward to the gurney.

"I can explain." Sam collapsed to sit.

Keltz stepped back. "No need. Answer a couple more questions, do not challenge my ability to detect crap and we'll wrap this up. How long has it been since you slept?"

Sam sighed. "I'm fine."

"I said no lies," Keltz barked. Emotion finally broke out on her face and the lady did not look happy.

"Ah… Maybe thirty-six hours."

"Do you wish to press charges against Miss Jensen for identity tampering and alias forging?"

"Absolutely not." Sam glanced at her. "Jenna, come here."

Keltz's hand rose and Jenna stayed frozen. "Was the contract you signed using the alias of Samuel Cooper nothing but a pretense to board that shuttle, and do you accept full responsibility for vows exchanged with the woman, formerly known as Laree Spring, who claims to be Mrs. Laree Cooper?"

Sam slumped. "Yes. I used her."

"Do you wish to renege on the contract as both Cooper and Dexter?"

Sam raised his chin and hope flared in his expression. "God, yes. Can I just pay some fine and a severance amount—I don't care how much—to be free of this? Of her?"

"You should care," Keltz muttered. "You'll be wide open to ongoing disputes without a clean, decisive break."

Jenna cleared her throat. "What do you suggest?"

"Man-up and keep it simple." Keltz narrowed her gaze at Sam. "Son, if you could control your fate for the next twenty-four hours, what would you want?"

"Honestly?" Sam shrugged. "A few hours of sleep without being hounded by anyone and legal ties severed with the woman I callously seduced and used for no reason other than the gut feeling something was—is—terribly wrong with a terrifying percentage of the bastards that run this world."

"In regards to the callous seduction, which woman are you referring too?"

Sam scrubbed his hand across his face. "Huh?"

"Not me." Jenna crossed her arms. "I was the one who tampered with his wrist phone to change his name so it appeared he was married to me then I drugged him."

"Hmm. Young lady, I have no doubts as to your integrity. His is another story." Keltz turned that cold gaze on Sam. "That's it? Rest and freedom from Mrs. Laree Cooper?"

Sam scowled. "Yep. Maybe throw in a glass of water," he blurted, "and a crown as I ask for world peace."

The woman resumed tapping at her wrist phone. "Before I crown you anything but presumptuous, you should reconsider leaving this facility without a bride on your arm."

"For the love of God, why?" Sam groaned.

Keltz glanced around the windowless room. "My mistake. Preoccupied with pretend illnesses and arranging sexual liaisons, perhaps medics neglected to mention this soundproof facility is surrounded by World Security. Seasoned soldiers, yet ill-equipped to handle mobs of lemmings wearing shirts expressing lust and admiration for a man they believe to be a romantic hero — erroneously? Time shall tell."

Jenna gulped as the woman's icy expression not only shattered, the hard glint filling the admiral's eyes had Sam flinching.

"One of those teenage idiots happens to be my child," Keltz said. "I'll personally see to your neutering and permanent incarceration, Dexter, if she's harmed in the slightest." The woman renewed working her phone. "But, on topic and deemed by the power invested in me as Attorney for the United Governments, the marriage between Laree and Samuel Dexter, a.k.a. Samuel Cooper, is hereby dissolved based on witnessed adultery — marriage amendment 808 stating that yes, oral counts — and my own dislike of womanizing liars."

Sam stared at the floor and the tightness in Jenna's chest returned with a vengeance. *Pretend-hooker, claiming to be sterile, erasing a wife and becoming one without consent. Round and round it goes.* If there was one thing she'd like in this moment, it'd be to disappear from this room, building and oh hell, why not wish she was on a shuttle for Jupiter?

Heavy silence filled the room before the admiral's flat voice continued, "Well, that's that. Unless you, Miss Jensen, have anything to say to or concerning this man who's not legally partnered to you either? Technically a bachelor?"

A bolt of anger charged up her spine. "Yes, I have an opinion. He saved thousands —"

"Blah. Blah. A true hero, yes. But on a personal level, what's your assessment of character?"

What on Earth did this formidable woman want? Jenna shot Sam a confused look. No help there. He sat, twisting the gold band on his finger. The one she'd given him.

"Strong, kind and a damn good man who" — Jenna swallowed hard — "I'd give anything to be married to and not just to easily exit this building."

Sam shoved to his feet as Keltz stepped forward, her intense gaze on Jenna. "Then you, young lady, you'd march this damn good man from this facility claiming he's yours in sickness and in health and subject to strangulation if he even attempts to consort with his fans or the press?"

Her heartbeat stuttered as Sam stumbled closer and went down on one knee. "Please, sweetheart, tell me I'm the happiest guy alive."

Bursts of joy yearned to explode within her, reined in by reality. "Sure." She drew a deep breath. "It makes sense to walk out of here with your head high and pretending to be married."

Sam jerked back. "No. Not a sham." He glanced at Keltz. "If she says yes, you can marry us right now? Make it legal?" He didn't wait for an answer. A grin broke out on his face. He pushed to his feet and tugged the ring off his finger. "Wow. I hope you can see them, too."

"See what?" Jenna asked. *Oh God, he's hallucinating.* Was he so sleep-deprived he didn't mean or quite comprehend a word he'd just said—her heartbeat stopped—that he really did want to exchange vows?

Sam clutched the gold band as he glanced about his head. "The bluebirds bobbing and rainbows circling." He smiled at her. "This is the real deal, sweetheart, if you want it to be. Love at first sight is an actual, for certain thing I feel for you, and not because we survived this first day we've had together. I do love you. I do. I do. And I want to say that again in front of the world."

Her throat dry, she pushed the words out. "You love…*me*?"

"I *do*." Sam gestured to Keltz. "Look. See that smile? She, the lady with the stare that shrivels balls, believes me. You should, too. Take off the ring, Jenna. Please."

*Ohmygodohmygod.* She tugged the band off her finger and tossed it as he did the same. The rings tumbled across the space of a couple of feet like the Love Center's logo, passing each other. Sam snatched hers and she caught his.

He winked at Jenna. "Maybe if I beg nicely, we'll get a first night together." He turned to Keltz. "Right, ma'am? Tonight?"

Keltz narrowed her eyes at Sam. "Do as told and we shall see. Keep those balls shriveled, put tongues back in your mouths and rings in a pocket."

The admiral's fingers tapped a fast jazz at her wrist phone. "I'd like an acquaintance or relative, who can be here within the half hour, to stand beside each of you as witness as required when not going off to colonize space." She looked up. "Names?"

Jenna pinched her arm. Was this happening? The brilliant man she'd dreamed about since she was a teenager, watching her with such passion, hope and love in his expression, was about to legally become her partner?

"I said names," snapped Keltz.

Sam jerked his head around. "Kurt...don't remember his last name. Guy who lost his wife and helped land the shuttle. He's around, mustering forces to break me out of here."

"And you, Miss?"

A haze of purple crossed her mind. "Um...there's a rep at the LC in this city named Lenard Harding."

Puzzlement crossed Sam's face while Keltz returned to dead fish mode. "The Love Center and all its assets, including employees, are stationary pending investigation, contracts within the past month automatically voided and fees to be returned."

Sam cleared his throat. "*All* contracts?"

"Yeah. Got a problem with that?" Keltz's lips pressed together, making a thin line.

"Manipulated into going down on my knee, and I didn't even need to beg to be released from the first Mrs.?" Sam cracked a grin. "Not in the slightest." He lost the grin. "Jenna... Someone at the LC?"

Heat flared in her face. "I'd like to find him. He'd be able to...ah...dress..." She peeked at Keltz, who looked up from her wrist phone. "Look, I have a right to ask for whom I want, don't I?"

Keltz glared at her, then dropped her gaze back to her wrist phone.

Jenna sucked in a deep breath. "Um...don't you think the press would agree a bride gets her way?"

"Hmpf." Keltz jerked up her chin. She looked as if she'd love to strangle Jenna. "I heartily disapprove, but per your wishes, Mr. Harding has been located. An agent is contacting him now." She returned to scowling at her wrist phone, and held her finger up, signaling Jenna and Sam to remain silent. A pause, then her low voice muttering into the phone was barely audible. "No. He's to come alone. I promise a court martial if this Harding isn't standing in front of me ASAP. Out."

Sam hadn't taken those deep green eyes off Jenna, and the bluebirds and rainbows he'd mentioned began spinning around her head as well.

# Chapter Twelve

Inside the chapel at the medical center, Sam stood at the front to the right of the pulpit. In all of a half hour he'd been showered, shaved, buttoned into a black tux and most importantly, had sucked down two large cups of highly caffeinated coffee. Kurt hovered beside him, wearing a forced smile.

"Sure you want to do this?" Sam mumbled.

"Do what? Put on hold plans to smash every suit I see who wants a piece of you, hang about while I marry — for real — the hot babe who saved my life, then bust out of here in a dramatic exit that'll have a gaggle of *In the Loop* fans either screaming with envy or swooning with happiness at the sight of a bride and groom who aren't en route to a funeral parlor?"

"Yep."

"Stop feeling sorry for me before I distract you with a fist to your gut."

Sam flung his arm around Kurt's shoulders. "We can postpone. Give you longer than a few hours to cope with your loss." He removed his arm and stared at the guy.

Kurt brushed non-existent dust off his lapel. He too wore a tux. "For the last time, I'm not fine but I'm here and I know I don't have to be. That medic would jump at the chance to be your best mate." He cracked a smile. "Hey, is it true you got to be alone with Jenna? Took the opportunity to get...blown away, divorced then down on one knee?"

Sam snorted. "Does everyone in this place know I got a BJ?"

"You're one lucky guy, Dexter."

"I am indeed." Sam's heartbeat stuttered. Low music, *Here Comes the Bride*, began playing and the most beautiful sight entered through the arched doorway thirty feet away. He barely glanced at the tall man in a white tux, taking in the short woman on the guy's arm.

Jenna wore a lacy ivory gown that swept the floor. Little frilled bits of silk were strung as accents everywhere, including places he couldn't wait to handle. The gown was slit from thigh to ankle so she could walk, and she looked so damn pretty that his knees were about to give out.

A low whistle came from Kurt and he grasped Sam's elbow. "Easy. He's something, that's for sure. Almost... Oh yeah, dear lord, I do wish I was gay."

"He?" Sam tore his gaze from the radiant woman floating closer and closer, and the guy escorting her stared right back. Thick hair—purple—reached his knees and fluttered about as he pranced forward, Jenna's grip on his arm, pulling her along. The pristine white suit had to be made of leather, molded to his lean body like a second skin and if a man cared, he'd find the muscular guy beyond movie star handsome.

A throat cleared to his right and Sam snapped his jaw closed. Admiral Keltz had come in the side door.

Wearing that impeccable navy suit, she waited at the podium.

"Get on with it," Kurt whispered and dropped his elbow. "Say something memorable before that dude — who looks at the bride like he's more bi than gay — upstages the groom."

*My bride. Jenna.* Sam swallowed hard. His heart pounded painfully as she came to a stop within arm's reach and smiled at him. He drew in a shallow breath, noticed and ignored the faint whiffs of a field of lavender emanating from the guy. "Nice dress." *Great. For a bibliophile who blogs for a living. I can be so lame.*

The man beside Jenna beamed. "It only is because a princess" — the guy had the nerve to wink at Jenna — "whose size I know well is in it. Best I could do with three seconds' notice. Did you know the beasts — took five ninjas — who kidnapped me wouldn't give more than a half a minute to grab that dress and a few necessities before they threw me into a — thank the stars — jet, not a shuttle?"

"Ahem." Keltz glowered at the man dwarfing Jenna.

"But enough about me." The guy matched Keltz's frown, his gaze steady on Sam. "I solemnly swear to go medieval on your ass if my girl ever loses that sweet smile. Understand?"

Jenna kicked Harding in the ankle.

*His girl? Over my dead body.* "You work for the LC?"

"Oh no, dearie. Not anymore. Their politics, crimes are unforgivable. Beyond awful. Seems I was hired for bigoted reasons. You know…the fact I'll not add to the population. I'd thought they'd wanted me because of my ungodly amount of natural talent." He shuddered. "Attempting to wipe out straights is so sick. Cold-blooded murders of poor souls who can't help their genetics. Horrendous. I could go on and on."

Jenna groaned. "Lav, please. Sam, Kurt, Ma'am, this is Lavender Harding."

Sam reached out and Harding took his hand. Firm grip. Didn't let go. Well, two could play this game. He tightened his clasp. "So you know Jenna how? Related?" *Tell me the woman I've known for three days has a gay brother with lilac eyes.*

Harding squeezed, released Sam's fingers and smirked. "No. Met her merely hours ago. She fell hard for me, my skills."

Jenna's blush deepened.

*Christ, she didn't want her mom or a girlfriend, but some stranger to stand by her?*

"And mate," the guy went on, that intense lilac gaze ranking over Sam, "I guess your jealousy has foundation. I do have deliciously naughty incestuous feelings for the sister I dressed to please a reckless, selfish, attention-loving activist who almost got her killed."

Sam drew back, guilt and anger seizing him by the throat. He parted his lips —

"Shut your mouth, Dexter," Keltz grumbled. "I carry a licensed handgun. Any male who says anything other than 'Yes' or 'I do' in the next five minutes is getting plugged. Dearly beloved, we are gathered here yada yada. Samuel Dexter, do you take — "

"Yes." Sam shot his left hand out toward Jenna as Harding dropped the gold ring in her hand.

Two minutes passed in slow motion until...

"You may kiss the bride."

He did. *Mine. All mine. Until I die.* His arms eased tighter around Jenna. His mouth on hers went from gentle to gonna-rock-you-all-night-long, and his dick didn't hesitate to hurtle the hardness scale while his heartbeat drummed with pride.

Too soon, Kurt grabbed his elbow and Sam cracked open his eyes.

Harding, *the bastard*, had Jenna's arm and kudos for husband partially lifting and holding to wife so they could maintain contact as the men guided them toward the exit. Sam's feet moved as if they trod on clouds, and he deepened the kiss. His lungs began aching, threatening to burst. He'd forgotten how to breathe through his nose, and forgotten to ask someone to rebind his ribs.

He didn't care. He was never gonna let her... Harding, *the damn bastard*, pried them apart. Jenna stumbled and the long-haired man swung her into his arms.

Kurt took one side of Sam, Thomas grasped his other, and he went up onto their shoulders. A pair of WS — World Security — uniforms hurried them down the deserted corridor and into the bustling lobby.

Medical employees clapped and cheered, *double damn bastard*, at Harding and Jenna. The pair were dressed in matching white, the train of the dress draped over Harding's arm, Sam's bride ducked her head against a broad chest and rode in the guy's arms as if she weighed as much as a toddler.

Kurt and Thomas burst out laughing at Sam's sour look. They strode faster to catch up with the couple moving out the doors flanked by security, letting in the roar of an excited crowd. Shrieks bombarded his ears. It looked like hundreds, make that thousands, were pushed behind electronic ropes that could be set to either knock a man on his ass or cause permanent cardiac arrest, cordoning off a path of a hundred feet to a waiting chopper.

Young women wearing bright T-shirts with — Holy Christ — X-rated versions of the blog's name across their bouncing chests squealed Sam's name and ogled Harding.

"Oooh, look at his hair."

"Such a cute couple."

"He's so hot."

"Best butt — ever."

Wrist phones were clicking frantically and a realization hit Sam, harsh and below his self-absorbed belt, emphasizing he was an overtired idiot. Harding not only carried Jenna to spare a celebrity with battered ribs, he also shielded a loner who'd spent the past decade avoiding the public eye. The Net would be flooded and software used to confirm identities. Any minute, it'd leak that the slumped man hoisted by friends behind the charismatic man blowing one-handed kisses to the crowd and shielding Jenna's face, was the actual groom.

*Fuck-fuck-fuck.* Why the drawn-out publicity show? What was taking security so long to punch Harding, so he stopped screwing around and hauled Jenna onto that chopper? The skin prickling between Sam's shoulder blades became a horrifying itch. "Put me down," he snapped.

"Be cool," Kurt said as he and Thomas lowered Sam to his feet. "She's not gonna fall for..."

He tuned the guy out and glared, gesturing at the nearest security — too late. Fear scrambled along his spine as the unthinkable happened. Jenna did fall. Directly from Harding's arms as he bent, staggered and dropped her.

Through the din, Sam couldn't hear any sharp crack to herald further shots — better aimed and to the head — but he anticipated. *Christ, Please-please-please.* "Get down," he bellowed and lunged. Jenna was scrambling to catch her feet, twisting toward Harding, who had crimson splashed across the white leather pulled taut by a muscled back. Sam plowed into that back—purple hair ruffled as bullets flew past where Harding's head had been—knocking the injured man down on top of Jenna. Harding yelped and went silent as Jenna cried out, smashed into the sidewalk beneath them.

Hands seized his shoulders. Kurt hefted him up to his feet and security swarmed in a protective circle. Two lifted Harding—limp with eyes closed—off Jenna and another grasped her, shielding her with their armor-protected bodies. Sam began breathing again as he noted she appeared dazed but unharmed.

The crowd stared, shocked into an eerie silence. That changed as heads swiveled upward toward the roof of the medical center and the figure dressed in black falling from the skyscraper. People yelled and gasped. Those in the way scrambled aside as the body landed, bounced and hit the concrete pathway, again to remain motionless.

They'd taken out the shooter, but the drilling band of tension circling Sam's skull didn't lessen. The men hovering around Jenna hustled her for the chopper. Security carried Harding by his shoulders and feet the opposite direction, back for the medical center. Sam opened his mouth but Kurt beat him to it.

"No, no. If he's alive, he may not be for long inside there."

The two agents paused. Sam barked, "On the chopper," and the pair reversed course, carting the downed man to board behind Jenna.

Kurt turned to Thomas, who looked toward Harding with a deep frown on his face. "There'll be a med-kit on the aircraft. Can't you come with us?"

Thomas gave an abrupt nod, and Kurt and Sam ran to hop through the wide hanger door, the medic on their heels.

A man and a woman sporting brown government uniforms sat in the pilot seats. The two men in the silver colors of the WS, wearing impenetrable and lightweight armor, settled Harding on the chopper's floor, and yet another WS agent guided Jenna to the bench along the side wall.

The pair who'd carried Harding jumped out of the chopper, leaving one WS member onboard. As his gaze locked on the woman in bloodstained white, the smooth lurch, a sinking feeling in his gut and the change in noise of the rotating blades told Sam they were airborne and rising straight up.

He staggered to Jenna's side, sat and grasped her hand. "You're okay, right?" Tears on her cheeks, blood on her hands and red dots sprayed across the front of the dress. So much for the first few minutes of married life to a notorious informer.

His bride didn't answer, just stared at the long body sprawled on the floor eight feet away. Thomas and the WS guy were all over Harding, who lay motionless on his stomach, head cushioned by a blanket. They'd cut off the leather shirt, and Thomas pressed a compress below the shoulder blade as the security agent shoved a mop of purple hair aside to examine the side of Harding's head.

"Think he'll make it?" Sam asked.

Jenna swallowed hard, her body trembling. "Yeah. Because of you. Those bullets barely missed his head. Well, one may have clipped him but the blood is from his back." She jerked her gaze to Sam, eyes wide with shock. "How'd you know?"

"Know what? That some assassin thought your friend was me?" He mocked a scowl. "If Kurt and Thomas weren't holding onto me, I'd have tackled that lavender freak the moment he picked you, *my* wife, up. Who is he? Why—"

Jenna slapped her hand over his mouth.

In the olden days, before he'd become a criminal, he'd have respected the inalienable right of women to shut him up. But not this woman and not this day, when he should be the one mauled by medics. He pulled Jenna close and forced her hand aside. A simple shift of his tired arms and she sat on his lap, his hold unbendable and his hand covering her mouth.

"Look, it's none... Yes, it is my damn business why you wanted some hotshot movie star type who works for the LC that you've known almost as long as you have me at our wedding, but can you explain why? What about parents?" He eased his hand off her mouth.

Jenna stared, her eyes glazed. "He was kind to me. I felt—feel—a strong connection and my parents are dead. No siblings. No friends who'd believe me. Sam...is Lav dead? Because of me?"

He bent to brush a kiss on her ashen cheek. "I'm sorry. Soon as we can, I want to know everything about you, including instant friends. He's just a friend, right?"

"Yeah. Unlike you, I wasn't even married before—"

He slapped his hand back over her mouth. "Kurt?" he called out. "He... Jenna's friend, is he okay?"

Kurt shuffled forward to crouch in front of them. "Clean shot through the shoulder. Looks to me like he'll be fine."

"Head wound?" Sam watched Thomas apply some sort of spray to Harding's temple.

"Just a crease. He's still out because Thomas sedated him."

Jenna heaved a deep sigh of relief. Sam released her mouth as the woman in the brown uniform marking her as government stepped from the cockpit. Kurt straightened and grabbed hold of a roof drop support while the woman thrust a wrist phone at Sam. "Admiral Keltz wants a word."

"Er... Why doesn't she use my line?"

"Deactivated, along with those of the other civilians on this aircraft."

Sam arched his brows in puzzlement.

"The general public hasn't yet been protected against the TandB virus," the woman said.

"TandB?" Jenna wiggled and he reluctantly eased her off his lap to the bench.

"Tag and Bag." Kurt snorted. "My...wife, Linda, her brother works in criminal tech. He filled me in. It's a new way for killers to keep their hands clean, thanks to long-distance murder. A coward who has access to the PC — personal code — number, and can buy this seriously expensive software that tracks the signal from the last outgoing message the victim makes can even plan the timing so the vic about to have a fatal heart attack is in the locale they wish."

Sam's jaw sagged. "How's that possible?"

Kurt shrugged. "The electric current is bundled in the virus that's programmed to call and lock onto the signal from the last call from that PC number. Assuming the victim is aware of this virus, the killer can also play with him or her. A preliminary dose creates a pathway as current rides up the arm and into the chest. No outer cellular damage, a bit of a sharp tingle and not enough to fry the phone yet.

"The vic thinks what the fuck, starts to remove their wrist phone, but then the second jolt hits. It rockets on the already-conditioned path, powerful enough to toast the heart of a child or bring a fit man down. The third burns out his wrist phone, taking away any means to trace the incoming viral tag and guarantees he won't get up. Takes about ten seconds. Can also be done through a com-desk."

*Christ. The world we live in.* "Is that true?" Sam glowered at the agent.

"Afraid so." She sighed. "Government employees have constantly updated antivirals. Been told they haven't gotten a handle on price to provide for the less targeted general populace." She pushed the phone at Sam. "Ahh... The Admiral's waiting. She's... Well, it's *not* a good idea to piss her off."

His heartbeat steadily drumming in his ears, wondering if he was about to become smoking hot, Sam activated the phone for widescreen visual and full volume audio.

Keltz looked as deadpan as ever. "Dexter. I want your cooperation. Go online the moment I disconnect. Explain you owe your life to mistaken identity, that the odds are such luck as that shan't happen again, and you need everyone's help locating culprits." The admiral's eyes glittered. "There are over a thousand LC affiliates on the list I'm sending you—two hundred or more still at large. The attachment is programmed to accept upgrades. If a line goes through the pic beside the name, they've been apprehended."

"You want me to post, hoping readers will provide tips on whereabouts?"

"Obviously," Keltz said in a dry voice. "Direct them to the links in the margins of the alphabetical list. Billions are logged into *In the Loop*. Mere thousands on United Government sites. We need the public's help."

In other words, narc on neighbors. Create even more distrust and anger within households reeling from loved ones either dead or suffering survivor shock. But if these LC employees aided those who'd devised the means for mass murder, the least a whistleblower could do was help clean up the aftermath. Sam swallowed hard. "Understood." *I guess.* "Where are you taking us?"

"A stop and drop at a secured medical facility to unload Harding, then coordinates for a rooftop within proximity of a safe house will be sent to the pilot. ETA in fifteen."

Secured like the last medical center was? Sam glanced at Kurt. Off view of the phone's monitor, the guy shook his head.

"I want to stay with Lav," Jenna told Keltz. "Until he's awake and not in any danger."

*There goes the honeymoon. Again.*

"What's his status?" Keltz asked.

The WS man unpropped his tall, muscled form from the wall beside Sam. The guy hustled over to Thomas, who bent over Harding, perhaps checking his pulse, then hurried back. "Medic says he'll be out for hours."

Sam plastered on his dopey grin. "Why waste a minute to land, hover over the medical center and toss Harding out of the chopper? That'll wake him up."

Jenna matched Keltz with the eye roll. "Apprehending conspirators is top priority, Dexter. I expect your post viral. Immediately." Keltz disconnected.

Sam stared at the phone coiled in his palm, a sleeping eel about to wake and snap down on his pulsating wrist. Once he entered passcodes, they'd be sure to flash on a screen in front of Keltz, no matter what privacy laws said. Any working phone on this chopper would be compromised.

The government agent arched her brows. "Hit the attach-app and upload." She smiled. "My name's Lander. Want help?"

*Duh. Like I haven't been on the Net before I could walk.* He ignored her, turning to Jenna, whose grip on his arm had grown tight enough to cut off circulation.

"A thousand LC workers?" Jenna murmured. "Many will likely prove innocent of anything other than being oblivious or looking the other way. Outing them to an incensed public…? Well, don't you think that'd lead to vigilante justice?"

"My wife's family wants blood." Kurt scrubbed a hand across his eyes. "Can't say I don't feel the same. But Linda's dead. Nothing can change that. Beating or killing employees of the LC who may be as clueless to the puppeteers pulling their strings as I was, won't help me sleep any better. Plus, giving opportunity to any liar with an ax to grind is rather whacked."

Kurt glanced at Harding's collapsed form and shifted his brooding gaze back to Sam. "Here's a paranoid question. Since when do our leaders ask a blogger for help?"

The agent—Lander—drew her head back. "Whoa. He's got a point. Couldn't the admiral spam everyone like the governments usually do?"

Sam's heart sank. "Using *In the Loop* to advertise a list of bad guys gives credibility. Fans who trust the blog— trust *me*—will have specific faces to focus their rage on."

"Yeah." Kurt snarled. "I bet addresses and last known whereabouts are in the fine print beside the pics. And…take these suspicions a step further?"

"You're wondering if this rescue is a sham." Jenna twisted her fingers at her side, grasping at the blood-spattered gown. "That we, key witnesses, are about to die, as hundreds of potentially innocent employees of the LC are torn apart by mobs?"

"Is something wrong?"

Sam startled. He hadn't noticed Thomas leaving Harding. The medic hovered too close to Sam, a concerned look on his face. "Better hurry and do as the admiral said. We arrive at a medical center in ten." Thomas smirked and slapped Sam on the shoulder. "Then I hear you, my man, are on to an exclusive hotel that provides toys, pills, all that. Despite the most comfortable beds on Earth, you'll be up," he winked, "and hard for as long as you want. The least you deserve is a proper honeymoon, right?"

*I deserve to get fucked in comfort?* Entitled because he'd survived and gotten the girl. Sam's stomach clenched as anger flashed across Kurt's face, and a blushing Jenna ducked her head. He'd been thinking with his dick since he'd stepped into that bar. How could anyone lose sight that this day — supposed to be the happiest of their lives for thousands of couples — had been the worst?

The medic's wide smile turned sickly. "We're almost there, Sam. Enter your codes and I'll load the attachment while you kiss your wife." Thomas glanced at Jenna and shrugged. "And if she doesn't change her mind, wants to stay in hospital with him," he gestured at Harding and continued talking to Sam as if Jenna wasn't sitting right there, "I'll fight off all that pussy dying to take her place. Keep the bed warm for her." He rested his hand on Sam's shoulder, the bad-boy leer returned to his face. "Hey, after you're done posting, let's check out pics of the shuttle landing. Amazing how fast those young tangs got shirts printed."

Sam jerked away. His jaw dropped for the umpteenth time. *Crude bastard. How many people am I gonna want to kill this day?*

"How'd you know about the list?" Lander bristled at Thomas, reassuring Sam he wasn't the only one who wanted to punch out the medic. "You couldn't hear us talking."

Thomas stepped back. "Yes I could. What's your problem? You want in his bed, too? Well, bite me, sister. A lot of competition, but Dexter isn't a fool. Can't imagine any guy would want to fuck a brown coat on a day like today." He shifted his glare from the government agent to Sam. "Upload already, will you?" Thomas spun on his heel and returned to crouch beside Harding, his back to them.

Lander drew a sharp breath and whispered, "He's been using his phone and he's on it now. That means…"

"Like you, he's government," Kurt growled as Lander narrowed her gaze at him. "Not saying you're in on this, but he must be. He answers to that admiral. We're screwed. In the air and about to die. Again."

Sam stiffened. His chest ached, every bone and muscle including his heart. *Balls. I'm so stupid.* It'd all been too easy. Getting alone time with Jenna, manipulated into thinking exchanging wedding vows had been his idea. Keltz had played him for a lovesick sap.

Then, worst of all, concluding Harding had taken bullets meant for him. The shooter had only failed at two things — a lethal shot and getting away. The flaws in the scheme for Sam to blindly sanction who'd go down for crimes was Jenna knowing a LC employee, and not eliminating Harding at first attempt.

Why else sedate a gunshot victim with a possible concussion? Keep Harding unconscious but breathing so the rest of them remained calmly clueless, then get rid of the employee once he'd been isolated, so Harding couldn't protest to Sam that he knew people on that list who were as duped concerning the LC as he'd been.

*Balls.* What if Harding wasn't breathing? Murdered while they sat watching? He bounced to his feet. "Get off him," he bellowed at Thomas and hurried forward. In a burst of rippling silver, the WS man stood between Sam and the medic. The guy seized Sam's arm.

Thomas straightened from his crouch, and raised his angry gaze from his wrist phone. "Goddamn idiots. Forty seconds left."

"Until what?" Sam jerked his arm but the silent security wouldn't let go. "You kill that man?"

"Does it matter? We're all dead, you imbecile." Thomas groaned. "That blog post isn't live in thirty-nine seconds and this chopper will be nuked."

Sam's heart stopped. The WS man released him and Sam raised his hand, the wrist phone still clasped in it.

"Come on, Dexter. Please," cried Thomas.

"Don't do it," Jenna called out. She stood between Kurt and Lander, both grasping an arm, and ten feet away from him. "The good of the many…"

*Oh Christ.* Sam unclenched his fingers and the phone fell. Before fate snatched him from Jenna forever, was there time for a kiss goodbye?

A powerful hand seized him. A police-issue, steel-titanium handcuff snapped round his wrist. One arm shackled to Sam, the WS guy punched Thomas in the face, knocking him back into the wall. Without taking his gaze off Thomas, the man retreated, pulling Sam with him and blocking the others behind them.

Blood spurted from the medic's nose. "Assholes." Thomas barked a laugh and tapped at his wrist phone. "I was gonna save you, Dexter."

The hanger door began opening. A row of chutes—six—dropped from the ceiling along the wall behind Thomas, and the sunlight glittered off the blade popping out of the medic's wrist phone. The bastard cut and slashed at the chutes, grabbed up three and lunged away from WS-man and Sam racing toward him. They clutched air as Thomas ran out of the chopper.

The wind battering his face, Sam peered from the doorway to see a pair of unopened chute-packs falling past Thomas, who was tumbling and working his arms into the third.

The WS guy jerked him back from the edge. Guess the stoic dick preferred they'd roast, instead of merging with the ground. Sam twisted to stare at the three chutes left. "Kurt and Lander—move," he yelled. "Jenna, grab a damn chute. Ten seconds!"

WS-man didn't say a word. He pulled Sam to Harding, bent and grabbed Harding's arm and dragged them both backward for the hangar door.

*Three chutes—friend, wife, young woman—it's all good.* Sam didn't struggle.

"No," screamed Kurt, while Jenna stared at Sam from those beautiful and stricken brown eyes.

"Sorry, Jenna. I love you." He stepped backward, fell into brisk nothingness, and swallowed his scream against the sharp jabs of pain as his body bounced about. It felt as if his arm would yank from the socket. *Ah well. Maybe I'll have a fuckin' heart attack before losing my arm and going splat.*

# Chapter Thirteen

*Helpless. I failed.* Her heart feeling as dead and frozen as her limbs, Jenna watched Sam disappear into space. His black boots flipped up, his body following after the WS bastard who'd dragged Lav to his death as well. She couldn't move or even sob as the obvious solution to the fact the bluebirds, illusion of happy-ever-after, wished to stir once again within her numb brain.

*Screw until death do us part. He's* my *husband. Mine.*

Lander gathered up the wrist phone Sam had dropped while Kurt pawed at the chutes. Horror filled Kurt's face. "Goddamn him. Two of these are slashed." He held up the only good chute and made to toss it to Jenna.

"No," she snapped at Kurt and turned a beseeching gaze on the woman. "My life just died. You go. Hurry."

Lander didn't bother to speak. She shot forward to yank the only functional chute from Kurt, staggered back a couple of steps to thrust her arms in it, and threw herself at the angry man to push at him until both their bodies tumbled out the doorway into space.

*And I stand alone.*

*As I came into the world, thus I shall leave.* A foot from the edge, Jenna stared out into the pale blue sky. Time had to be up. She should brace for explosion. She snorted to herself. If her life was about to flash in front of her, why not relive the best bang she'd ever had? Embrace the memory and die with a smile. Her lips curled upward as imaginary arms took hold.

*My arms round his neck, his back to the wall, cock pounding in and out, hard and slick, making me feel so alive. He drills harder and faster, winding me tighter and tighter, then the hardest and fastest thrust puts him so deep taut balls slap my butt and I rocket with him.*

*The mere memory makes me wet enough to douse a heat-seeking missile, right?*

*God. I'm gonna die.*

How she wished she could really feel Sam holding her.

Strong arms grasped her from behind and she yelped. "Sam? You're a ghost?" *Wishes do come true!* She went off her feet, swept into powerful arms, and brisk wind kissed her face as the man leaped out into the sky. She flung her head against an unfamiliar male chest, and a massive sound — painful roar — blasted into her ears. Heat and jolts of fire surrounded her, singeing her legs and arms. Chunks of burning debris, flames reached for the billowing dress as they went down in a terrifying rush of freefall.

"Hold tight." The bark of a stranger's voice penetrated the harsh ringing in her ears. A large hand cupped her head, unable to ease the disappointment crushing through her. The guy holding her was not the right one. *Sam's dead. Like I wanted to be.* She blinked hard, taking in the brown fabric pressing against her face.

A government agent — the pilot.

The man released her head, supporting her with one arm as he clutched at the straps holding the chute to his back. The chute rippled up and blasted open as burning chunks of chopper fell about them. Heat snatched at her, bathing her, and a horrible hope blossomed in her chest. Good chance she'd still follow after Sam. Be incinerated, along with the fool who'd risked his all to help her. *I hate myself.*

A tug of the pilot's hand on a rope and they swirled to the right and downward, away from the wreckage. The bite of the wind lessened as the canopy puffed out and she sobbed. Nausea swirled into her throat. Specks, bits of metal debris pinged against the thin material of the orange chute sheltering them. Their descent smoothed. Instead of plunging, they began floating down.

She sobbed again and the man drew his head back. "Stop that. You'll be fine," he rasped.

"D-d-dead. He's dead."

"Look." The pilot angled, dipping and bending their bodies farther to the right. Beneath them was a pair of orange umbrellas, two intertwined bodies hanging under one. The third canopy was opaque and silver. The center figure wore the silver uniform of WS-man, and he held a long body clutched one-handed to his chest. A third man had one arm wrapped around the man's thigh, his other arm reaching up to clasp hands with the guy he clung to. The three fell fast, drifting past the chute with the couple and heading toward the solitary figure almost to the ground.

She gasped. "That agent had a chute?" *Sam's alive!* "Security saved Sam? That's Sam and Lav?"

"Has to be. Hang on." The pilot dipped his head, peering below. "Gotta bring us down faster before we drift into...obstacles everywhere."

She clung to the arm wrapped around her chest and followed his gaze to the tops of sparse trees, hundreds of pointed skyscrapers with lethal steel peaks, and people bursting outside doors from every direction. They looked so tiny, scurrying about and staring up. The pilot began fussing with straps, and the graceful float went back to the breathtaking plunge.

The crowd grew closer and closer, the wind whipped at her dress, stirring up the smell of burnt silk, and her head pounded from the intensity of the relief filling her. Assuming the security guy had been strong enough to support two men without dropping or crushing them on impact, Sam should be on the ground by now. She couldn't see the other chutes, her vision caught in a tunnel as they fell in a direct descent, and she braced for painful contact.

The pilot held her securely when his boots hit not tree, building or person, but concrete. A rough stumble, manly oomph, but he landed with the grace of a falcon carrying a heavy load.

The sheer material of the chute billowed around them, wire-thin straps attached in a grid pattern to the corners, and she realized she'd been rescued by an experienced jumper. If only Sam and Lav were as fortunate. Not face first, impaled on a building, crushing a small child…

*Sam-Sam-Sam. Must find him.* She pushed at the pilot's arm and he lowered her to her feet. The ground swayed but she held her balance — barely — as orange material tumbled over her.

Sweat beaded on her forehead as she tried to step out from it. The damn dress was designed to glide down an aisle, not maneuver out of a parachute. Orange fabric spun up and away. All sizes of hands helped, the rushing noise in her ears subsided and she became aware of the surrounding chatter.

"Oh my God, are you okay?" *I am now.*

"What happened?" *Dumb question.*

"Need a medic?" *God, no. Hope he's dead.*

"Move aside. Let go of me. Get the fuck out of the way." *Is that…*

"Sam? Sam—"

Sam seized her, his hands feeling warm and familiar, and his deep green eyes stared down at her.

She pressed into him and blurted, "Oh God. I thought you were dead. Then falling like that… You're all right?"

He winced. "Yes. No. A touch sore. My arm"—he tightened his grip on her—"feels fantastic now."

"Let's keep it that way," the pilot said. "We need to get somewhere out of the open."

"Thanks for saving my wife." Sam loosened his hold on her and stuck his hand out. "What's your name?"

"Welcome." The men shook hands. "Tim Lourde. My own wife will be glad I'm not collateral damage—yet."

"You want escort to a medical center?" a voice called out.

"No," snapped Sam, Jenna and Tim at the same time.

"Where's the others? My co-pilot, Lander?" Tim asked the crowd.

The array of anxious faces surrounding them turned. People stepped aside and a long splash of purple hair came into view. Lav looked either unconscious or dead, carried by two men. Another pair of guys held the elbows of the silver-suited security man who was moving slowly. Lander and Kurt took the lead. No sign of Thomas.

A young woman eyed Sam then glanced uneasily over her shoulder. "Black sedans and suits are closing in." She glanced to another woman at her side. "We can take them to our place, right?"

The older woman blanched. She refused to meet Jenna's gaze as she muttered, "Er... The kid is home. I'm not sure." She jerked her chin up. "It's not safe. I'm sorry."

A stocky, middle-aged man scurried forward. "I can help." He dragged his gaze over to Jenna and she tried not to shiver. The guy's grin widened as he turned to Sam. "Name's Cain." He jerked his thumb toward a nearby 'scraper. "That place is mine. At least part of the first floor is. Have a lobby area for my business — a law firm — and a connecting suite where I live. Struggling economy, I'm open only by appointment so the place is currently empty. You all could come in while the rest of these kind people form a barricade around the entrances."

Provide more bodies the government would have to explain if they attacked the building? *God, I love people.* Strangers willing to risk their lives. Jenna eased back, closer to Sam as the man — Cain — stepped forward to glance at their bare arms.

"No wrist phones?" Cain scowled, shaking his head at the atrocity of being disconnected from mankind. "At the least you'll have computer access and a chance to regroup. Maybe we can figure out what's happening."

Sam held tightly to Jenna's hand. Maybe he too noticed that Cain seemed a bit squirrely. Too eager. But the sooner they got off the street the better. "That'd be great. Thanks."

People parted, men slapping Sam on the back and nodding at her as they followed Cain into the entrance of a spiraling, thin 'scraper. Adrenaline and joy propelled Jenna through the double plated glass doors held open by multiple hands. No matter if thousands of soldiers stormed the place and made them all disappear or in this moment a missile was being directed to take out the entire block, she solemnly swore to herself she'd never let go of Sam again. The chatter of the crowd lessened as they entered the plush lobby, and he bent to her ear.

"I thought you'd died in that explosion. I can't... This is real. We're really here? Together?"

She stopped, peered at him, and her stomach clenched. *God, I could look at that raw stubbled chin, chiseled jaw, penetrating eyes and hot bod for a lifetime.* A sense of unreality filled her as well. She floated in a dream bubble that'd burst any time now. How could such a gorgeous man stare at her as if she held his heart in her hands? The obvious solution was to never let him close those eyes. After a good night's sleep, Sam Dexter might come to his senses and run for the hills.

He'd crash-landed the shuttle, hung to a man holding Lav—her unwitting friend who may be dead because he'd come to their sham of a wedding—while parachuting into a crowd, and yet Sam still looked so damn sexy her knees wobbled.

*Is he really mine? Wants to stay mine?* He arched his brows, obviously wondering why she stared at him with I-want-you-so-badly-sparkles in her eyes.

She swallowed hard and squeezed his fingers. "I understand how you feel. I too thought you were dead and never expected WS-man was so awesome." She glanced at the exhausted agent stumbling through the doorway. "Can't imagine the expense to make a silver suit not only insulated against bullets, but a chute compressed into the back of the jacket so perfectly, who knew it was there? And wow, to hold the both of you like that." Her breath caught. The second pair of men entered, carrying Lav by feet and shoulders. "Lav's still breathing, isn't he?"

"Was when we hit the ground." Sam started walking with her through the lobby after Cain, who was pressing his wrist phone to the lock pad of a door in the far corner. "But not even me landing on top of him woke him up. Our good friend Thomas had to have drugged him with something quite strong."

Sam turned, gesturing Kurt, Lander, Tim the pilot and the WS agent who'd saved Sam and was now helping Tim carry Harding, to precede them into Cain's home. He shifted that solemn gaze back on her. "Er... You said you've known Harding for a few days?"

"Nope. Few hours. But we never made it into a bathroom in a bar or a hospital room. Spent the time talking about this other man I met."

The blatant relief on Sam's face filled her heart. He chuckled. "Well, I can see why you like the guy. All that hair made a fantastic pillow." His hand wrapped around hers, he tugged her forward into the foyer.

The surprisingly spacious apartment held a small table and pair of chairs in a kitchen area off to the side. In the living room, easily double the size of her own, Kurt, Lander and the WS agent made a beeline for the com-desk.

"Kurt's on it," Sam said. "He and that agent will find some help that follows the Hippocratic Oath instead of their wallet."

"Come inside," Cain called out, and Sam and Jenna stepped into the living room. Facing the long couch they'd settled Lav on were monitors that covered the wall, sectioned into six gridded and muted screens. She cringed as an image of an intact helicopter from different angles filled two of the screens, and the aircraft burst into flames. Her name stood out in the print scrolling beneath the pics in seven languages.

"Balls." Sam glared as his image filled another grid. The feed showed him striding tall in his pressed pilot uniform, heading toward the shuttle wearing that cocky half-smile, as if he hadn't a care in the world. A stark contrast to how he looked now. Soot on his cheek and chin, black tux rumpled and torn under the armpit, he stared blankly at the picture out of dark eyes rimmed with exhaustion.

Jenna cleared her throat. "Kurt? You'll check with an online medic whether we should bring Lav somewhere or let him wake on his own?"

Kurt glanced from the desk area where he stood over the WS agent seated in front of him. "Yeah."

Cain didn't even look at Lav. Still wearing that cheesy smile, he stared at her as he approached her and Sam. "You both look exhausted. If you want to wash up, rest a bit, there's plenty of towels and a pair of robes in my bedroom." He snapped his fingers toward the hallway across the room. "Can't miss it. At the end of the hall."

Sam grasped her elbow. "Jenna?"

Kurt's head reared up. Blood rose in his face. "Er...shouldn't you wait here, Sam? This isn't over, you know."

Sam snorted. "If that's your polite way to say remain on guard, mate, instead of screwing around, I get it."

Kurt scowled. His brooding expression caught more than Jenna's attention. Cain outright laughed. "Lighten up," Cain told Kurt. "Let the lovers have their moment." He winked at Sam and muttered in a voice loud enough for all to hear, "Your friend there seems somewhat jealous you've a bride on your arm. Not my business but—"

"You're right. It's not," Sam snapped. "Kurt, Reese — you want me and Jenna to help?"

The WS man, whom Jenna gathered was named Reese, looked up. "Go on. Two hours. We've enough eyes on this."

Sam nodded while Cain turned from them to approach the group huddled around his desk. "I swear you're all safe." The guy shrugged at Kurt. "Sorry. I wasn't thinking. Let me make it up to you. I've got a bottle of Jack with your name on it. Come tell me what happened while I get some food…"

Jenna stopped listening as Sam bent to her ear. "What do you think? *Carpe diem?*"

Of course Cain was thrilled to have a hero in his home. The identity of the person who offered shelter, despite the long arm of the LC, would be all over the news, Cain applauded as a kind and brave man. Why not take him up on the offer to get in a shower?

Warmth bursting in her chest, she squeezed Sam's hand and smiled. Chin down, Jenna felt everyone staring at their backs as she and Sam hurried from the room.

"Be warned," Sam whispered as they walked down the impressively long hallway. "I aim to regress to a teenager. If they nuke this building, I want you to die happy."

*But I already did that. In my imagination.* And now, in reality, she could have her husband hold her on a real bed. Nope, she couldn't get any happier. Her breath caught as Sam stopped in front of the last door and scooped her up into his arms.

"Your ribs," she protested.

He grunted. "I'm fine."

Heat pooled in her stomach, pings of happiness escaping from her in the form of a nervous giggle as he toed the door open and swept her into a bedroom. The neatly-made double bed with a blue coverlet was centered in the spotless room — no visible cams and the window curtains were pulled closed.

"I found and lost you too many times to not seize the moment," Sam said. Two strides and she tumbled onto the bed. He stood over her and yanked his arms out of the jacket. It hit the floor. He unbuttoned the rumpled dress shirt, flinching as he shrugged it off and took note of the sweat stains. "Could you stay like that while I rinse off? Two minutes?"

"Sure," she lied. "But make it one minute."

He unbuckled his pants, heading into the bathroom. She swallowed hard, staring at the most perfect man she'd never fully seen unclothed — and damn well would as soon as possible.

The sounds of running water rang out. She pushed off the bed to her feet, and soon realized there was little choice if she wanted to shed the skintight burned and tattered gown without taking ten years to figure out how to reach the zipper without dislocating her arm. She grasped the corners of the bodice in each hand.

*Fuck. What the hell do they make these things out of?* The material wouldn't rip. "God damn it," she snapped and pulled harder. Last time she ever wore a bloody dress. "Oh Christ." She gasped to herself as it dawned on her that the adjective she'd used to describe the gown was literally true. The bright white bodice was speckled with Lav's blood, as well as black smut.

"Hey. I *told* you not to move."

She startled at the stern tone, spinning to face Sam standing nude in front of her. Water drops clung to every lean, muscled bit of him, including nasty bruising all round his chest. Her gaze raced south to halt midway down his long body. In all its mouth-watering glory, his cock hung plump and heavy. Turgid and growing harder and thicker as she eyed him.

"What's wrong?" he murmured.

Not a damn thing that she could see. She felt her cheeks flushing as hot as the rest of her body as she jerked her gaze up. Sam scrubbed his forehead, pushing wet hair from his eyes. "Jenna?"

"I can't get out of this stupid dress."

A large smile burst across his face. He closed in to twist her around. "That's intolerable. And, sweetheart, much as I liked that pink thing, I sure hope the way this dress hugs you, there's nothing but you underneath."

His fingers brushed her neck, sending electric jolts into her chest as the zipper went down and he peeled the gown off her shoulders. She heard his breath hitch as he looked over her shoulder at her breasts popping free. Like it had a mind of its own, his cock jutted out to press into her back.

All doubts, insecurities whether he wanted her as a fast fuck, a sweetheart, a wife, went poof in a rough gust, comparable to a chopper being blown out of the sky, as Sam groaned and wrapped his arms around her to clasp a breast in each hand. "You are so beautiful." He squeezed gently then harder, running his thumbs over her nipples. "Thank you for granting my first wish. Let's see if my second will come true as well."

"What wish?" she squeaked. His cock jerked against her, working the silk of the dress between her legs, and if she could have her heart's desire in that moment, she'd become six inches taller and he'd jackhammer those seven to eight impressive inches into any hole he wanted. From head to toe her flesh and bones hummed with the chemistry she felt for the man trailing his hands down her ribs. He bent and began kissing along her spine.

"No bra. Now I pray for no panties." Hands on her hips, he pulled back and fell to his knees. His face pressed into her lower back, he kissed her bare skin and trailed his tongue down as the torn and dirty silk fabric deserted her, taking all cognitive thought with it, other than how much she wanted him inside her. Little kisses and nibbles became exhilarating licks and she moaned, her legs trembling in an effect not to push against him. He eased his head back, dropped his hands from her hips and lifted one leg at a time to free her from the shambles of the wedding gown to leave her as nude as him.

"Ohhh Lord," he murmured. "Sweeter than I imagined. You know, this is the first time I've had chance to look at my wife's butt?"

She straightened, shivers running through her as he groaned and clasped her hips, twisting her away from the dress and around to face him. "But you don't want vanilla or anal sex in a stranger's house." He guided her backward. "So, my turn to snack." He stopped at the edge of the bed and brushed his finger along her cheek, rubbing at soot or blood?

"How do you know what I want?" she murmured, her heart racing.

His hands froze. "Tell me."

She tugged loose. "Okay. Don't move while I hop in that shower."

He scowled. "No. It's a standard bathroom stall. Plenty of room for me and a peanut-sized girl. I want to scrub, kiss, touch…taste…"

She stalked away, smiling as he went silent. She wished she dared to exaggerate the swing of her hips as his gaze drilled into her backside. No question, he breathed like he was a man who liked what he saw, and her entire body tingled with anticipation. "I know exactly how big you are. Be right back."

"Shower together or not, I'd never do anything you don't like."

She stopped, but didn't turn around. "Look for a condom," she whispered. *God, hope he knows we'll need a truckload of lube as well.* "Vanilla could turn into chocolate or any of a zillion flavors, and I...might...could...*do* want to try them all. You up for that?"

"Sure," he groaned and she heard him falling backward on the bed. "I'm as up as a guy can get, but it'll take a lifetime."

"Yes." She chuckled and walked forward. "Lives end in a blink. I won't waste a second more than I need to wash Lav's blood off me."

"Okay. Hurry."

She scurried into the bathroom. Visions of that lean body and stiff cock waiting for her swirled in her head as she turned on the shower and stepped into the stall. Hot water pounded onto her face and breasts and she smacked the app beside the knob. Body lotion sprayed out, surprisingly clean and crisp-scented, and she took the fastest shower of her life.

She hurried from the shower into the dry blast of heated air, not waiting for it to do more than take the edge off her dripping. She didn't glance into the mirror, but strode as fast as she could back into the bedroom.

And halted. *Oh God.* He looked so cute. Sprawled on his back, thick cock nestled between his spread legs, arms out and eyes closed as his chest rose with the deep inhalation of a man who'd passed the stage of dozing into being pretty much comatose to the world.

# Chapter Fourteen

*Something's not right*, muttered the annoying dude — the devil — who was perched on Sam's metaphoric shoulder and stating the obvious inside his mind. A mind that agreed with eons of reasoning that if there were a demonic presence in the universes, it surely wouldn't waste dark energy by invading the dreams of a miniscule chump of stardust named Samuel Dexter.

*No shit*, said the equally grating voice of Logic. *Stuff happens when authorities have us trapped in a condo marked with a big red X.*

The devil snorted. *That's the gist of it. Nothing's happening. It's stupid to waste the lull in action by no action. Naked. In a bed. Get it up.*

*Shut it up*, snapped Logic. *Sleep is the closest to peace an exhausted brain — neurons all braced to be splattered to kingdom come in a hail of police bullets — can get.*

*Didn't we promise to love, cherish and make come in the wretched kingdom that's here and now?* The devil growled. *Asshole. Wake. Up.*

*Right*, said Logic in that dry, sarcastic tone. *Address the ass and ignore me, the neocortex? Fuck it and fuck you,*

*Dexter. Let Worry and Stupidity deal with your devil. I'm sick of trying to rescue a hopeless dreamer. I'm outta here. Off to find a Vulcan who appreciates me.*

The devil laughed as Logic threw up its lack of hands, exiting stage right, and Sam groaned, aware he did so in his sleep. The definition of insanity was dreaming of enduring verbal abuse within his thoughts as his mind tried to coerce his unhappy body to rouse.

So far, despite the increasing agitation within, the waking up thing wasn't happening. His fists twitched at his sides, his stomach muscles were knotted and his heartbeat uneasy but, damn it, he needed this. He didn't know where he was, why his legs dangled off the edge as if he lay on a little kid's bed and he didn't care. He just wanted to sleep—for a few years or so.

*Taking a nap in the middle of a war is the true insanity,* whined Worry, the relentless voice that Sam knew would drone on and on. *Where are we? Why aren't we in the bed right? Will our chest ever stop hurting? Hey! Someone answer before I explode our head. Where the fuck are we?*

*Our ass is on the end part of some stranger's bed after bailing out of the sky,* said Idiot, the nutter who thought being a spy slash terrorist was epic. *Parachuted from a chopper that got blown up. How cool was that?*

*Moron,* the devil chimed in. *The authorities have this place surrounded. Dexter, you know my game and my name is Sin. So if you want to have some fun before the curtain goes down, get with the program. There's needs – righteously deadly sins – to attend to. Got to find somewhere safe, then stuff face, figure out why everyone dotes on a purple-eyed clown who's much too into our girl for a gay man, wrathfully strangle an admiral, get a prideful blog post up –*

*Don't be me,* Idiot interrupted. *Sam, listen. Deadly sins can wait. We need to recoup and heal. John Q. Public is an effective barricade against the LC. Just go back to sleep.*

*No*, gasped Heart. *Wake up completely.*

*Great*, grumbled Devil. *Who asked any organs to awaken? Too bad I'm not real and holding a pitchfork. Heartburn, broken heart, ripped from the chest, I could go on and on.*

*Go spin someone's head*, Heart told Devil. *Sam, you gotta snap out of this.* She *isn't safe.*

*She?* bellowed Cock. *Where? On this bed? Jenna, I hope. Move this naked ass. Shift to the side. Let me see.*

Sam gave up. All hope of remaining unconscious, letting his body recover, would continue to be clobbered under the most powerful voice in a clamoring sea of desires. He could always count on one deadly sin to outshout the others.

Now that his dick had sprung to life, any sort of slothful sleep was history. No matter what his stomach had to say, Gluttony wouldn't even get to taste a couple of strawberries, assuming some sweetheart placed a bowl within reaching distance. Wrath, Envy and Pride didn't stand a chance.

*Oh God. Hang on*, gasped Blood Cells. *Here we go again. Rushing south the moment the big stiff scents the air.*

*Love me, do me, fuck yeah, yeah, yeah*, sang Cock. *Pump me up, you little fat hemoglobin cells. I wanna come, come, come —*

"Quiet," Sam snapped.

"Sam…?" murmured a sweet, sleepy voice from too far away. "You're awake?"

Thank Christ, the question was too rational to come from within his squirrelly head and it had the desired effect. The weird brain activity flatlined, silenced by loss of blood, the rise of dick and the voice of an angel promising heaven somewhere just above his head. Sam pushed his eyelids up.

The ceiling of the stranger's bedroom staring down at him was awash in shadows, lit by one dull light by the door. He blinked, craning his neck toward the slender shape lying higher up on the bed. It looked like about a thousand miles of sheet separated them, a problem he'd fix at once.

Sam started to roll to his side, and all two hundred and six bones within him began to throb in protest. He remained on his back, slapped his palms to the bed and shifted upward until the top of his head banged into a pillow. He pushed it into the bed board and leaned back. His heart started beating again when the gap alongside him morphed into the most perfect curves.

He opened his arm — *waiting – waiting – ahhh*. So lovely, her eyes closed, face awash in sleep, the most beautiful woman in the world settled her head on his chest. Just like that the hurt behind his ribs disappeared. "How long was I out?"

"Ten minutes," Jenna murmured.

He clasped her closer. "Christ. Sorry. I usually only sleep five minutes every three days."

"Um…maybe it's been a few hours or so. Not sure."

"Any thoughts on how I can make it up to you?"

A small hand eased low. "I think you are up." Jenna brushed her fingers against the base of his cock and his skin quivered with delight. She fluttered her eyes open. "Shouldn't we see what's happening?"

"Outside of this room? Hell, no. I'm naked. You're wearing some guy's robe." He pushed at the material, slipping it off her shoulder so he could caress the bare skin of her upper arm. "Does this robe mean, you know, the honeymoon's over?"

Jenna laughed. "I sure hope so." She peeked up at him, then settled back and drew a deep breath. "There's a com-desk by the window. Before I fell asleep, I checked. No Net. I can't remember the last time that happened."

"Ten years ago." A shiver ran down Sam's spine. Problems with security had been traced to three different continents and a number of major dating sites. Shortly after the sites were shutdown, the LC took control on a global scale and since then the Net had remained deceptively stable.

"You think the people who helped us are okay? That it's over?"

Sam sighed as the weight of the world returned to his shoulders. "Much as I wish, it can't be that easy. But if whatever's left of the LC wants some payback, I think the missile would have hit this building by now." He eased his arm from around Jenna as his thoughts darkened. Could be, with hopes of being less conspicuous, anyone who'd helped him was being taken out one by one and they were saving the most wanted for last.

Jenna shifted her head from his chest and lay back beside him. "Lav. Kurt. The man who owns this place whose name I forget—what if they're not asleep but in trouble?"

"Cain, and no. Harding's probably still combing his hair. Kurt would have woken us."

She snorted. "Cain?"

"Guy who let us have this bed."

"Ahh. But maybe Kurt…"

"Shh. I'll go see if the world's still spinning." He made to move his feet to the floor and halted when he felt the clutch on his leg.

"You're leaving me in the dark?"

He was no dummy, so he knew better than to reassure her by gesturing to the nightlight in the ceiling. Besides, it was a reasonable assumption this heroine spoke metaphorically. She figured he'd not return to mention the armed men outside the bedroom door in this eerily quiet hideaway. That he'd just disappear. Good chance she was right, but in case the tremble in her hand on his leg was actual night terrors—and who wouldn't have whacky dreams after that chopper ride—he reached to search for the control panel on the bed board.

The gridded section was there as expected and he tapped the first indention. Ceiling lights came on in each corner, enough to see some detail, but not the freckles on her pretty face. He could barely make out the smudges of exhaustion beneath lowering eyelashes, and her hold on his leg didn't lessen.

The next indention didn't bring more light, but the wall facing the bed turned into a monitor to show a muted movie—ancient pirate ship sailing on a turbulent sea—in progress. The bisexual crew was in various stages of nudity and intimacy in the background, the focus on a young woman wearing a three-pointed captain's hat and nothing else, pressed sideways against the helm to give full view of the muscled ass of the hulky man drilling in front, and the ecstatic face of the sweaty man pumping behind her.

Sam tore his attention from the screen and tapped to turn it off. He homed in on the next level on the grid. The first indention raised a short panel alongside the side of the bed. The size and positioning looked about perfect so a guy could easily roll and line up his cock. He guessed it was an expensive condom dispenser. In the age of sterility and ease of making sure a partner was clean of STDs—anal sex participants aside—it was somewhat comforting to know he wasn't the only non-gelded guy left who liked the added reassurance of government-issued rubbers.

His next taps of apps offered a box of tissues, lube, then finally, a light in the shape of a sun filled the far upper corner of the wall alongside the bed. On the opposite wall, a cheerful field of irises and sunflowers had soft lights hidden within their faces.

He turned and brushed his finger along Jenna's cheek. "That better?" he murmured. "I'll be back in a minute. Want me to turn the movie back on?"

Her nails dug into his leg. "Don't you dare."

"To what? Movie or leave?"

"Both. Not that I've watched many pornos, but I hear the plot never changes, just like horror films. The moment lovers separate is when the loon bursts in with the ax."

"Okay. We'll face the bloodbath together, when you're ready." Like he'd done it every night and morning of his life, he leaned against the pillow, wrapped his arm around her and placed his palm on her hip.

She blinked her eyes open and released his leg. Her hand slid up to rest on his upper thigh, close enough to make his cock go from stiff to so hard his head fogged.

She stroked, the tips of her fingers firm and confident, along the sensitive area where his leg met his groin. "Hope there's no cams in here and Cain's not looking to get rich. I saw all those T-shirts outside the medical center." She smiled, dragging her gaze up and down his throbbing cock. "It's not only the LC that wants you."

An awareness struck him. On a comfortable bed with a hot babe, of course his body was completely awake, but so was his mind. After days of non-stop action, banging his chest into the console of a shuttle, catching a couple of hours of uneasy sleep, he was no longer even groggy. Appetites — lust taking the lead — bubbled beneath the surface of his thoughts, yet none of the urges clamored with aggression.

He reclined, balls achingly taut, pre-cum eager to bead out of the slit on the tip of his cock, his leg muscles tense and ready to take charge. He could easily roll over her, raise himself up and use his knee to spread her legs and get on with some serious fucking. How was it possible he wasn't already inside her?

Maybe because he knew if that door burst open and his balls were still harder than diamonds, he'd die happy because of a simple truth. *She's mine. My wife.*

No matter marriage no longer held the commitment of ages past—saying "I want a divorce" was as simple as saying "will you marry me"—he relished this moment. Shortly, her hand resting beside his cock would decide if they'd either make love, or walk out that door to face the world, for better or worse, together.

He'd never felt like this before. Not with any other person. Comfortable in Jenna's presence as if he'd known her all his life, yet his cock so primed it was likely he'd soon come just from looking at her. As her eyes closed, a bashful lowering of thick lashes, he smiled to himself and wondered if she felt the same.

"Like I said, everyone wants you," she murmured. "Alive and out there, making sure lovers everywhere remain safe. They all wish they could thank you in person. Some more enthusiastically than others. That's the only reason we're still breathing. You get that, don't you?"

*Yes and no, and who cares.* He cleared his throat. "It's true that I have the ear of the world because of a blog. But I'm only the current heart-throb getting those five minutes of fame because I haven't had chance to update and clarify who the real heroes are. And so what? I'm off the market. Forever."

"Wow. Forever? You sure about that?"

"Absolutely."

"Sam...are we really married?"

He jerked his chin up. "Damn right. It's not about a contract or some proclamation by a corrupt admiral. You're mine. My wife. I mean...I want to be with you. I feel like we're a bonded pair."

"You're happy?"

He glanced at his yearning cock. "Yeah. And not just the obvious part of me. What about you?"

The sweet smile creeping across Jenna's face stole his breath. "Yes. So happy. Except I watched you fall out of that chopper to your death and I wanted to die."

He patted her shoulder. "It's over. I'm fine."

"I don't want you to be just fine." She went in for the kill. Her soft hand wrapped around the base of his cock to encircle his girth with a loose grip, slamming the air from his lungs. "I want to see *the* moment on your face."

"Ohhh yeah." He gurgled as her clasp tightened and eased upward. "That feels so good...ahh...the moment?"

"You know...your O-face? It's so beautiful. And if this room is about to fill with security or the LC decides that shutting down *In the Loop* is worth taking out any number of civilians, well, twice isn't enough."

"Beautiful? And here I thought I showed the manliest expressions." He chuckled. "Christ, Jenna. I love you." He drew a deep breath and grabbed the top of her robe, yanking it open. Her breasts exposed, his breath hitched as he lowered his mouth to hers.

Gentle, easy, savoring—oh no, not his girl. Jenna was having none of that. Her tongue shot in, insistent and hungry. He pressed harder against her mouth, sucked and pulled the taste of her into his own. His senses flooded, the noise of his rapid heartbeat rushed in his ears, and he ground his cock into the soft fabric of the robe he needed her out of and fast.

He stopped loving her mouth with his tongue, dragged his lips aside and swallowed his pant. A soft moan fell from her lips as he licked down to nuzzle at the dip, the hollow at the base of her throat. He shifted his hips, forcing his cock aside, and used both hands to spread the robe wide.

"Sam…"

His head humming, he tongued her belly button and shot his hand down to widen the space between her legs.

"Sam…"

He jerked his head up. "Sweetheart?"

"I can't see your face."

"Missionary, then?" He slid both hands under her butt, pulling her up to his lowering lips. "Sure. One taste, then whatever you want. I promise."

Hair trimmed, the soft mound so beautiful, pink lips glistening—he licked, lapped then sucked. Jenna moaned, arching up, and he went at her full steam.

It didn't take but a moment before her breathing grew raspy. He took a last lick, raised his hips and homed his drooling cockhead in to rub and kiss her clit.

"Saaam…" she moaned. "Come on. Come with me."

"Ahh… Should I use a condom?" He licked his lips, the crème, her taste something he planned on savoring again and again for as long as he breathed.

She jerked her head back. "Oh. Right. You didn't mean it…when you said…"

He worked his cock harder against her without entering, slipping and sliding in their juices. "I meant every word. I just wondered if, you know, we should plan things." He held her still with one hand and grasped his cock, guiding it to grind against her clit.

"Be responsible?" She groaned. "And I have to decide while you're touching me like this?"

"No." He chuckled and released her. "Maybe we shouldn't tempt fate. Let things happen as they will, when we're not on top of the world's most wanted list?" He took in her softly open mouth, gaze on his cock as he shifted for the condom dispenser, to mean she was fine with whatever as long as he got back to it at once.

Somewhat squeamish, considering this wasn't his bed, he lined up his cock without touching the panel. The heat sensors within the metal plated grid registered the presence of an erection, and the red light in the corner showed he'd activated the dispenser.

Programmed to selectively heat seek the blood-pumped tissue of a penis, four nozzles the size of needles shot out and sprayed.

In less than two seconds, he'd been coated up and down and all round with skin-tight, biodegradable, government-approved sheathing from cockhead to base. Not an insecure guy, he eased aside and made sure the red light flickered off. He believed the warnings that filled condoms may require medical assistance to remove on idiots who messed with more than one coating to increase girth. Of course, the protection hindered some feeling. Nothing was as good as going bareback, but it did the trick and it was easy to peel off a solitary layer, twist and dispose, without leaking a drop.

"Ready?" he murmured as he rolled back into place and smiled down.

"Oh yes." She raised sparkling eyes, lids heavy with anticipation, and he didn't think he'd ever been happier in his life. She held her gaze locked onto his as he penetrated, slid in a tantalizing inch and halted. He lowered his head and readied to go in for a kiss of her breast.

"Hey…" She squirmed and his balls went impossibly hard. "You know what I want to see." Jenna lunged up onto her knees and wrapped her arms around him. He eased back onto his haunches, pulled her down onto his cock in one deep thrust and stared into her eyes while he took her lips with his.

They exchanged gasps, sucked down each other's warm air, and rocked together for a wonderful moment until Jenna tore her lips from his and drew in a deep breath. Her muscles clamped around his cock and his lungs locked. "Better not bruise those ribs any further." She pushed at him, shifting her weight to ease him over.

He fell flat and his gaze never left hers as she rode him, using her knees to raise and lower herself. Love, pleasure and hedonistic joy of living in the moment filled her face. Most interesting, as he grasped her hips and helped her power up and down, the look of bliss told him those emotions mirrored from his gaze right back at her.

When his balls drew up, pulled so tightly he thought they'd splinter, and he tipped beyond that level of even pretending he could hold back, it crossed his mind how much he wanted married life to never end.

# Chapter Fifteen

Stars slowly stopped going supernova inside her mind, and Jenna melted into a blanket of gratified flesh as she slid off Sam to lie beside him. His eyes were closed and the quiet contentment on his face had to match hers.

He opened his arm and she tucked into his side, curled toward him and brushed her hand gently over his chest. Now that the room was flooded with light and his cock rested sleepily against his thigh and wasn't distracting her, she took a good look at the discoloration and bruising across his ribcage.

*I'm such a selfish slut.* But who'd blame her? It didn't seem possible the most cynical of man-haters wouldn't start drooling the moment they saw this body, let alone heard that raspy low voice or got off from reading his cognitively and emotionally stimulating blog posts.

"Sorry. I keep forgetting your ribs." She caressed his abdomen, tangling her fingers in the beautiful trail of dark hairs. "I should have made Thomas tape them back up — before he turned evil, I mean."

"Shh. I'm fine."

"Liar." *I wonder what brilliance is obsessing his thoughts right now.*

"Am not, and I can prove it." His eyes snapped open. The breath caught in her throat as he bent his chin to stare at her. "I can't stop thinking about what you said before you jumped in the shower."

She tilted her head, blinking up at him. "Remind me."

"That you wanted—insisted on—trying every position in the Kama Sutra as soon as possible."

"I said that?" She dropped her head back. The heat—blazing light—in his deep green eyes sent warmth rushing south, cueing the moisture to flare between her legs yet again.

He smiled. "No. But that's what I heard, and brace yourself, sweetheart. I can easily come up with a thousand more positions than the sixty-four in the original translation."

"Is that right?" she drawled.

"Pick one. Any angle you fancy. I just need two minutes."

"You're gonna kill yourself."

"I accept that and surrender my free will." He stroked along her arm. "Fate's Bitch, that's my name. If I die right now, in any position including this one, I'll go out a—"

The door flung open and the question of whether to fuss further or take top before he could, went haywire in her mind. Kurt stormed in with the owner of the condo, Cain, on his heels. To her surprise, they were dressed in the silver jumpsuits only WS agents were allowed to wear.

Sam startled, sitting up. "Hey. Ever hear of knocking?" He blocked her with his shoulders as she joined him to sit, and began frantically shoving her arms into the robe that lay beneath her. "What's with the get-up?"

"Sorry." Kurt came to a halt in front of the bed and raised his arm.

Jenna stiffened. The edges of the robe fell from her trembling fingers. He held a weapon. Some sort of handgun.

"What the—?" Sam went quiet.

She twisted to see his head snap back. The scream filled her throat as Sam collapsed, giving her a glimpse of specks of blood edging the small hole—centered in his right temple—before the back of his head hit the pillow.

Her jaw dropped. Her entire being in denial, she didn't register the implications of much except she hadn't heard a pop or bang. Silencers had been banned for over a decade. She spun her gaze from her lover's vacant expression in time to watch Kurt take aim again.

Searing hurt ripped into her chest. A sharp jab that lasted a long second before her limbs—all of her—went numb. She could no longer feel the bed beneath her or her own head slapping back against Sam's chest. His rigid, unmoving chest.

*Oh God, he's dead. Really dead.*

*No, no, no. Kurt—how could you?*

*Sam. My husband. Mine… And why aren't I following you?*

She felt nothing. At least not physically. Emotionally, the first stage of grief hit so hard a voiceless scream of this-isn't-happening burned hotter and hotter, searing through her mind, while her body remained immobile. She couldn't speak, couldn't move a finger, vocal cords unable to articulate the despair roaring inside her without an outlet. If tears spurted from her eyes, they fell on cheeks too numb to tell. Her gaze was frozen, fixed on the ceiling, her head unable to turn and eyelids unable to blink.

All she could do was see….maybe not. The howling inside her mind, the rushing keening of horror that she leaned on her dead lover continued, but there was also noises outside of her head. Harsh male voices.

*My ears work? This can't be real. It just can't.*

"Christ. They're both dead? For real?" It was Cain's voice. Seemed he agreed with her.

*No, not again. Sam can't be gone.* She lay flat, paralyzed and staring at the spackled ceiling.

"That wasn't the agreement." It sounded like Cain was close, in front of the bed. "Him yes, but not her. Not yet."

"If you don't believe your eyes, go buy a damn PFP," Kurt said. "Probably an app on that expensive com-desk of yours."

"Will do, boss. Amazing how many gadgets you can get instantly if the price…" Cain's voice faded.

PFP was the acronym for a tool, the pulse-flatline-probe. A thin rod, the size of an old-fashioned pen and a medical device for determining death by inserting the needle tip into an artery. She'd shiver if she could. Kurt's voice sounded so cold—as if he'd never hugged and slapped Sam on the back at the wedding. No emotion from the guy who'd sat by Sam's side in the cockpit of that shuttle. He, honest to God, had killed Sam and done some sort of bizarre, paralytic thing to her?

Well, Jenna doubted that'd last long. Another bullet would finish her off as soon as the men figured out she was a cognitive vegetable. A man, a so-called hero for his role on the shuttle and not connected with the LC, murdering Sam and her didn't make sense. Kurt had lost his wife, his bride. Had he snapped? In a jealous rage because they'd found happiness? Then he'd forced the guy who'd offered sanctuary to assist him?

The answer to the last question became clear when Cain's face abruptly loomed over her. No fear, concern, or grief in his expression. More like disappointment. "What a shame." His gaze was downcast—on her breasts. He licked his lips then smiled. "Can't feel a thing pumping at her neck with my thumb. She's got such a dainty neck. Hey—you know how to use this PFP? Just jab it in I expect." To her relief Cain's horrid fake smile moved away. "If there's gonna be squirting I'm tapping the femoral instead of the neck."

*Please-please-please. Get him off me.*

"Give me that thing," snapped Kurt. "Keep your filthy hands to yourself."

Cain yelped as if Kurt had smacked him. "What's your damn problem?" Cain barked.

"Touch her again and I'll show you. Got at least eight more rounds." Kurt's face reared above her. A flash of white in her peripheral vision led her to think he'd grabbed the robe and yanked it closed, covering her breasts. Then he was gone.

"What?" Cain whined. "You promised I could do her and ice her myself, and why's it matter now? She's dead."

Kurt snorted. "This weapon uses thirty-sec ammo to flatline a normal brain. That means it should turn an idjit brain into soup in ten seconds. Want me to test it?"

"Calm down." Cain groaned. "You're scaring me."

"Just have some respect." Kurt had lost the robotic tone. His voice was now low and hard. "Pawing either is necrophilia."

*I'm a corpse and so is Sam?* The anguish churning inside her, the desperate certainty this was nothing but a sick dream, made it difficult for her to follow the conversation.

"Well, yeah. But not like I haven't seen every inch of both of them." Cain's cheerful tones made her want to vomit. "The vid fee will do lovely. My ticket to a better life." He laughed. "I got a look while you played hitman for the LC. Better than any porno on the market."

"Shut up. Don't talk unless I ask something. Where's those body bags?"

"By the door. I'm going to own an island. Once the public — all those fans — understand that's Dexter, I'll make millions auctioning off each frame. First, a head shot. Then a close-up of that cock when it's not so limp. Then her riding, cowgirl style."

"Not if I destroy your com-system." The sound of Kurt's angry voice went distant and returned. "Pull the sheet over him and bag him. Hurry."

"In a minute. Haven't had a chance to check the other feed. I love how you dropped then lumped the bodies. Real cold. Speaking of temperature — hope you look as hot in that uniform on vid…" Cain's blithering faded.

*I slept in the bed of a bisexual, porno-loving mercenary. Billions on this planet — why'd we have to parachute to land beside such a monster?*

But no matter how awful the diabolical stranger who offered them shelter was, Kurt's betrayal was unfathomable. He'd seemed like an old soul she'd known all her life, similar to how she'd connected with Lav. Someone she'd felt she could trust and care about from the moment she saw him helping in the shuttle, then sprawled on the aisle floor, back to a pod and weeping with his dead wife in his arms.

Both men had gone silent. If she could feel or see, she suspected Kurt's dark gaze was burning into her still form — or maybe he stared at Sam. Was the man happy? Licking his lips as he too imagined the payoff from murdering Sam, then sharing his most private, final moments with the vultures?

"Excellent," Cain called out, loud and excited as if he spoke from the other side of the room by the com-desk. "This fuckin' smokes. The look on their faces — on yours. Good thing the LC promised us new faces. We're gonna need them once the bidding war goes viral for first copy of this, as well as the sex. Great snuff stuff. Just fantastic. The WS man, pair of government pilots, the man-candy LC employee, all wasted. Real time deaths caught with elite, HD lenses will — No...stop!"

She heard a rough gurgling and Kurt snapped, "I took out the two most admired people on this planet. You don't get Dexter into that body bag — now — I'll up the count to include a spineless mercenary."

Cain gasped. "You prick. Let go of me then."

*Dead? They're all murdered? Ohgod-ohgod.* If only her heart could beat, it'd explode. She had to face the truth. This was real. No dream, no lack of physical sensation, could ever be this vivid.

But why hadn't she died as well? No pulse meant no air. It'd been more than five minutes since she felt the last thing she had, that harsh jab of something penetrating above her left breast. Her lungs didn't work. Even if the bullet hadn't done the job it should have, it didn't make sense lack of oxygen hadn't.

"Omph." Cain groaned. "That fucking hurts."

"Him. Bag *him*. Go near her again, I'll jab my thumb in your eyes and you'll whack off without visuals."

Her thoughts, the fear and confusion, ratcheted up to helpless terror as Kurt returned. His grim face moved back, taking her frozen gaze with him. That meant he'd slid his arm under her and lifted her as if her body wasn't stiff but limp?

She didn't have a clue when or if rigor mortis set in on a comatose person who didn't need a pulse to maintain consciousness. There was one small consolidation. At least she couldn't feel the touch of this man lowering her on top of what she assumed was a body bag. If her heart could beat, it'd pound hard enough to crack every one of her ribs. She wanted so badly to ask him why.

Kurt's face—eyes filled with remorse—closed in as tenderly as any lover. Close enough to brush his lips on her forehead? Then his mouth slid to her ear and he whispered, "So sorry. Wish you could hear me. But this will be over soon." He shifted back. His head dipped to look down at her, and the mechanical look returned. She heard the sound of the zipper approaching her chin—black filled her vision—and she lost her sight as well.

"Whatja say?" Cain's voice sounded muffled.

"Nothing. Stop dicking around. Carry Dexter out after I zip him. I'll get her."

A frightening realization hit her. Had Kurt spoken to her, despite thinking she couldn't hear, mean he knew she wasn't dead? He planned on dumping her in some grave? That's what he meant by over soon? *Oh God. Buried alive.* Was Sam just as paralyzed as she was?

In her mind's eye, her fists clenched and she swung. Without moving in the slightest, she imagined bashing Kurt's face in. That sound of enamel clacking on the floor was the noise his teeth made after falling out of his mouth. That drip of fluid splattering over her knuckles was her blood. Was any of this real?

*I can't feel anything.* She mentally wailed, screaming in silent frustration because she couldn't move her hand to slap herself into waking up.

"Why are you such an asshole?" Kurt's voice was muted, as if he talked through a mask, and she strained to hear. It wasn't easy eavesdropping while trapped inside the attire of a corpse, cheaply made and quite porous to increase biodegradability. Government issued and used for standard green burials or cremation shrouds as well as transport.

"No reason to bang him about like that," Kurt continued. "Unless you're too much of a sissy to carry him properly. He too heavy for you, little man?"

Kurt didn't want Sam's body manhandled, but showed no remorse for shooting them. Was this yet another sign the guy was vindictive yet seriously deranged?

The next ten minutes of quiet didn't do a thing to move her past denial and anger into the bargaining stage of grief. She had no expectations of some hero or a deity coming to the rescue and raising the dead, doing what was right. If she managed to somehow come out of this coma state, she'd do so with vengeance on her mind. *Ah, Sam, I can't believe I'll never hear your voice again. Not feel your touch. See your gorgeous eyes. Listen to and read your thoughts.*

It was a nasally whine—Cain's voice—that interrupted the suffocating feelings of loss and fury swamping her.

"Stop glaring at me. I'm a lover, not a coroner. But that's six bagged and waiting by the lobby door, including the famous bride and groom, and the LC isn't even here yet. What's your damn hurry?"

"You're really are a moron, aren't you?" Kurt sounded like he wished Cain was included in that count. "When the clean-up crew arrives—think they won't jump at a chance to add us to that pile? No payment. No chance of future blackmail. No further bad publicity with your perverted tapes destroyed."

"Right." Cain yelped. "Can't believe I didn't think of that. We need to get outside and surrounded by witnesses. Wait for me, okay? I gotta upload the films."

"Net's still down."

"Shit. Fuck. I'll pull the hard drives from the bedroom com-desk." Cain's worried voice retreated. "Be right back."

"I doubt that." She could barely make out Kurt's mutter. "Hopefully soon another bastard will roast in hell." Kurt drew a deep breath and raised his voice slightly. "Albert...Allen — whatever the hell your name is — come in. Door's unlocked."

"Jesus Christ," said an unfamiliar male voice a moment later. The man emitted a low whistle. "Look at them lined up and ready as promised. You okay?"

"No," Kurt snapped. "I'm not okay and I'm not gonna call you Jesus."

"Allen. I'm WS. Reese is my partner."

"Reese?"

"World Security, who saved Dexter and the LC employee in that chopper. You know, the man you stuffed in one of those body bags over there. On topic, the perv's in the bedroom, meaning we have a minute or two before Cain goes crispy or runs?"

"Yeah," Kurt said.

"Better haul ass then."

"What about Cain's security, his cams?"

"I'll take care of them if he doesn't activate the TandB virus, which will do the job for me. Give me a hand with this and start loading."

"That's a layered stretcher?" Kurt asked. "It'll hold all six?"

"You got it. Easier to deal with the crowd if we wheel everyone out at once. Maybe put her, the lightest one, on top."

A moment of quiet then one of the men gave a deep sigh close to her head. "You're not looking too steady. Need a hand?" asked Allen. "That's Dexter?"

"No. Got him and yes." Kurt groaned. "I keep expecting to get a whiff of charred Cain. The prick should have come out of that bedroom screaming by now."

"Maybe the Net isn't just selectively down as we figured, and the virus remains loaded and locked. Finish up. I'll go check on your greedy host."

A few minutes of nothing then Allen's voice grew closer. "No longer our problem."

"Cain's dead?"

"As if the chair, Old Sparky, was pulled out of storage. Monitor's frozen on zero. Countdown window reads — in effect, but minus the bullshit disclaimer — 'Virus infection. Get away or die'. By the burnt wire smell, the vid feeds are collateral damage. As unsalvageable as Cain is. Don't look so guilty. It's for the best. Hate to see Dexter's ass all over the Net. Cain could have heeded the warning. Taken his chances with us."

"The best? That stupid dick trusted me." Kurt's low voice was strained. "I...never killed before."

*Right. Had to go serial on my wedding day.*

"You didn't do Cain," Allen snapped. "Bet the pervert thought it was a bluff. And huh? Rumor says it was you that snapped a guard's neck on the shuttle."

A sound rang out like Kurt snacked himself in the forehead. "Oh God. I can't believe I forgot. It happened so fast. What type of man does that? Kills someone and forgets?"

*Ahh, what about Sam, Lav, Tim, the WS guy I never knew was named Reese and Lander, who saved your butt on the chopper?*

"A survivor who lost the love of his life." Allen grunted. "Postpone the meltdown. I was the one who set up the virus. Bastard's on me. And unless you want to join Cain, don't even borrow someone's wrist phone, let alone pop open a com-desk. Put your game face on. They — authorities at WS — know that virus hit here. We gotta roll."

A moment later a bombardment of voices came at her. Based on the muffled commotion, multiple people screaming out, she guessed she'd been wheeled out of the building and they were outside, surrounded by paparazzi.

"Is Dexter alive?"

"Who's in those bags?"

"Amateur radio operators say no word. Radio silence means the worse? Is it true…?"

A solitary voice — Allen's — rose out of the din. "I think this stretcher compresses to fit through the hover door."

"You don't know?" Kurt sounded quite close, an edge of panic in his tone. "Well crap. I forgot to read my 'how to stack corpses' manual before I went on my honeymoon. There's a handle. Pull it already."

"What about the lady on top?"

"She's small. She'll clear…I hope."

# Chapter Sixteen

The bastard *hopes* the lady on top of this stretcher will clear the doorway? Sam was furious he couldn't even unclench his jaw and respond to that. *Idiots. I need to kick some serious ass.* Laying on his backside in a coma, he'd never felt so impotent in his life.

Goddamn Kurt. Goddamn paralysis. Goddamn asinine escape plan that resulted in a bunch of fake dead bodies and one actual one. Ironically, they'd left Sam out of the loop, sleeping like a trusting babe, while they'd plotted and called in another WS guy who must have brought toys, such as a poison-laced weapon, with him.

Sam needed his chest to rise, to suck in a large gulp of air and the muscles in his throat to thaw. Not too much to ask, was it? To be able to scream at the assholes that fake killed him to make sure Jenna was okay. Once he could stop fretting about her, he'd concentrate on the rest of him snapping out of this drug-induced state of suspended animation.

He desperately wanted free of this suffocating body bag, then to wrap his arms around Jenna before he ripped Kurt a new one. How dense could the guy be? Kurt had chatted merrily away with Cain. Dumb fucker hadn't a clue that the pseudo-paralysis toxins he'd shot into them didn't affect hearing.

The whomp-whomp sound of an aircraft's blades remained steady, while the cries of desperate fans eager for his wellbeing muted. Sam would heave a sigh of relief if his lungs worked. Kurt hadn't muttered, "Oops, my bad." Sam had to assume the stretcher had fit inside the medic-hover without smashing Jenna.

"Where's the app to close the bloody doors?" a male voice bellowed. Maybe the driver. Sam had never ridden in a medic-hover before. Too bad he couldn't feel a bloody thing. A relatively inexpensive cousin of the helicopter, the hovers maintained a low attitude, barely clearing the 'scrapers, as they zipped across the sky, bringing victims to medical centers.

"I don't know." Kurt spoke close to Sam's head. "Forget the doors. Get us in the sky before *In the Loop* nutters break the barricades."

"This junk hover won't lift with the doors... Ah...here we go."

To Sam's mounting frustration, he didn't notice a sense of motion, a lurch upward telling them they were airborne and fleeing the LC. Again. If only he could lift his arms, claw out of this bag like he had the pod on the shuttle. First thing he'd do was strangle Kurt. Or, if he'd been turned into a zombie, he'd choke then eat the brains of his best man — assuming the guy had any.

Shortly after he'd shot Sam, Kurt had whispered in his ear, "*Dang, too bad you lose all senses when puffered. Poor bastard. Can't hear how sorry I am about this crazy stunt.*"

Obviously when they'd come up with this idiotic means to get Sam and Jenna out of the public and government sights, Kurt had gotten his facts wrong. Despite complete muscle paralysis, Sam could hear, see whatever his eyes were aimed at and he could damn well spin his wheels.

Just like he assumed Jenna could. The innocent sweetheart he'd allowed to board that shuttle was certain to be freaking out. Didn't seem possible she could be in the loop on what puffered meant.

Years ago, after he'd typed tetrodtoxin and frog in the same sentence for a potential blog post, his wrist phone had chimed. An older, sinister-looking man with a chest weighted down by silver stars had given Sam the riot act concerning informing the masses about potential biological weapons. After thinking it out, he'd had little choice but to agree with Big Brother. He'd stopped researching and found a less problematic topic to chat about.

Pufferfished had to be the military's slang term for a state of false death. What he'd learned before backing off was that toxins from a fish he'd thought had gone extinct could be combined with tree frog and toad venom. Add in some sap, an infusion of the Datura plant, and the white lab rat was shown—ninety-some percent certain—to collapse and begin decomposing with no chance of rising. No zombie mouse shuffle after the dosage wore off. Pretty much certain there'd be a grave to lay flowers on for Algeron.

From what he'd understood, the Puffered Project had been closed down. He should have known better. Man's ego to prove he could do something, no matter how senseless, never ceased to astonish. And here Sam lay, living proof all those dead mice had eventually paid off so scientists could give authorities, mainly World Security, yet another weapon to keep from the common criminal.

Sam guessed his current pulse and respiration was so low only a medical device could show he wasn't a corpse. That'd be the reason Kurt had made sure the PFP, the tool to show positive death, had stayed out of Cain's hands.

The idea of a means, in bullet form, to let your enemies think you were brain-dead seemed incredibly stupid to Sam. Competent killers wouldn't trust an accomplice to be the one holding the medical probe. Or they'd grab a serrated blade and remove all chance of being deceived by slit throat and decapitation. So far it seemed unlikely science had figured out how to pull a Frankenstein.

All these minutes — going on an hour, for Christ's sake, of being a vegetable — able to do nothing but brood, was beginning to seriously piss him off. Speaking of Christ, would Sam have to wait four miserable days like Lazarus had? *Come on, Kurt. Jesus me back to life already.*

Any mad scientist worth their salt might have come up with something better than a time interval to shake off a fake-death toxin. One pill makes you the living dead. Another jump-starts you back into the land of being able to punch a man in the nose.

Finally, he heard someone clear his throat. "Hey, Allen," Kurt called out. "I didn't get all the details. Too busy plotting with Cain. How long until they can see and hear?"

"What?" Allen barked.

"Sight and hearing returns before movement, right?"

Allen snorted. He sounded like he stood beside Kurt and the stretcher now. "Wrong. Only three senses are affected. Breathing's way too shallow for smell. Taste requires throat muscles, and of course touch is screwed.

Muscles and nerve endings are paralyzed. But vision and hearing are fine."

Kurt gasped. "You're telling me that Sam…all of them can see inside those bags?"

"And hear."

"Why wasn't I told that?" Kurt snapped.

"Look, I just did what my partner said. No time to coddle, especially you, the guy pretending to be in cahoots with the LC and that greedy pervert Cain. Who do you think sent the virus? Yeah, I initiated it but it was a stone cold hitter at the LC who had the juice to do the nasty. The LC has been royally screwed not once, but now twice by Dexter and his best man."

"I get it," Kurt mumbled. "But…bloody hell. We're standing next to six conscious people listening to every word. How long until they regain control? Shouldn't we unzip those bags? Where are we taking them?"

Allen groaned. "Civilians. I should have let Reese take a dummy bullet. Then he'd have to answer… You hear me, man? Reese—you dumb fuck, hang in there. I'll stick you in two secs. Baxter, what's our ETA to the drop?"

"Twenty," bellowed the man Sam assumed was piloting.

"Any tail?" Allen yelled back.

"Not yet. Looks like the decoy hovers are taking the heat."

*Come on, Kurt. What's the deal to wake us?*

"Stick your partner?" Kurt asked. "With what?"

"Concentrated dose of epinephrine. He'll either die for certain or jump up with fists flying. Back at Cain's place, Reese expected his bullet to be a dud. But if you're going to put on a show for authorities, it should be done right. Not like he…like *you*, Reese, can act worth a damn."

"Just get them moving so we can unload faster," the driver yelled. "Less conspicuous, too. Their transport is skittish as it is."

"I concur." Allen lowered his voice. "Here — syringes. In case Reese doesn't die and is whaling on me, bring the others around. In the chest, over the heart. I'd leave the injured LC employee for now. Not sure how stable he is."

To Sam's relief, it seemed there was an end in sight to this darkness. As expected, Kurt chose him to stab first. He heard the zipper coming down and his unblinking eyes saw — a steel grid. The top of the section of stretcher was only a few inches from his nose — and tilting away.

Kurt's face loomed over him. The guy held him in his arms, lowering him to the floor. "Listen, buddy," Kurt said, "keep it together and don't frickin' die on me, okay?"

*Wouldn't dream of it.* The low ceiling of the cramped medic-hover was made of two inch by two inch gray tiles. Kurt's worried gaze shifted aside, and if Sam could have held his breath he would have.

He didn't feel Kurt's hands on his chest or the needle going in. Hearing took the lead of the sensations bursting within him. There was an abrupt explosion of rushing-pounding in his ears as air slammed into his lungs. Grayness, the color of the walls, blurred his sight. Black dots swam in front of his eyes. His throbbing chest heaved. His heartbeat jackhammered so hard as he sat up. The pain of the tachycardia swallowed the scream galloping up his throat, replaced the bashing hurt against his ribs with rage.

Fists clenched, muscles now so taut they ached, as stress-induced hormones surged. Fight or flight response nailed him, in overload. The metallic taste of too much adrenaline exploded up from his stomach to coat his throat. He knew the snarl twisting his lips couldn't get more primal. He blinked hard and his vision cleared and he saw red. He barely registered Kurt wrapping his arms around his shoulders. Trying to pat him on the back like he was a boy waking from a nightmare, not a man in full warrior mode — out of control — in a killing rage.

"Fuck," Sam gasped. He thrashed his arms out, shoving Kurt aside.

Kurt reared his head back. The man's lips were moving but Sam could no longer hear. His erratic heartbeat was so loud, he wondered if his eardrums were rupturing. He shook his head, clearing splashes of blood red fury away, and spit the words out. "Go. Away. Before I kill..." *Forget fighting like a man. Regress to flight. I'm a caveman. With a wife to protect.* "Jenna!"

"Easy, mate, easy. Just breathe." Kurt inched closer and flung his arm back around him. "Kill me later. After you wake her."

That made sense. And it felt awesome, to be able to feel the sensation of someone holding him. Sam sucked in a deep inhalation then exhaled. And again. To his relief, the crash of blood roaring in his ears began to subside. His heart rate lowered from gladiator-surrounded to just-ran-a-marathon.

"Jenna..." His forehead was coated in moisture, his vision blurred again.

Kurt released him. "Yes, yes, of course. Quit screaming. I'll get her for you."

Huddled on his knees, Sam grabbed at the blue sheet wrapped around his lower body and lowered his face to drag the edge across his cheeks. Tears and sweat streaked the linen. He raised his head to see Allen — the new WS guy — sitting on a sprawled Reese on top of the body bag. Reese's skin was gray, sweat dripped from his chin. "Get off me, you dick," Reese bellowed. Most likely as loud as Sam had called out for Jenna. He twisted his neck, looking...

"Sit tight and keep breathing," Kurt told Sam and shoved to his feet. "I'll get her down."

"Overdosing on adrenaline" — Allen winked at Sam — "puts a man in a tizzy." He eased off his partner and bounced to his feet. "Get it together, Reese. Help me babysit the pilots. I'll take the pretty one."

By the tall stretcher wedged against the hover wall, Kurt gently pulled the body off the top. A moment later, three people lay on the floor. Kurt watched Sam unzip Jenna, while the WS guys crouched over Tim and Lander.

Sam looked into Jenna's unblinking eyes. "It's gonna be okay, sweetheart. I'm here, holding you. In a second or two you'll feel me." Sam tugged the robe slightly open, nodded at Kurt, and Kurt pushed the syringe into Jenna.

Kurt scurried aside as Sam gathered his wife — chest heaving, gaze wild — into his arms and sat back on his haunches. Jenna didn't come around swinging. But it took what seemed like forever for that frantic heartbeat to slow, his murmuring to penetrate and her chest to heave in deep breaths instead of shallow, frantic gulps.

"Sam...I... Oh God. You died. Again. Have to...stop —"

"Shut it," the driver snapped. "Listen up, folks. We're approaching the unload point."

Jenna quieted. She burrowed into Sam as the rough male voice overrode the panting and gasps coming from the two government agents.

"You've got a minute to decide if you're sticking with World Security or if you're going to risk it all in WITSEC."

"Witness protection?" Kurt grumbled. "Might as well fall on our knees now and eat a bullet."

"Don't be stupid. You think the WS is any safer?" Baxter's authoritative voice from the front echoed off the narrow walls. "Allen, Reese and me will have our hands full saving our own asses. Allen—get those duffel bags—clothing for those we're dumping off in two minutes."

"What's the deal?" Kurt stood, hunched in the low hover, staring at Allen.

Sam held Jenna tighter and jumped in to support his best man. "Who'd be hiding us and do they know the risks?"

Allen arched his brows. "Unsanctioned help and used only in cases of extreme emergency. Set up by agents I trust. And yeah, they agreed once they heard your name. No hesitation. You all damn well better be polite to these people, too."

"Huh?" Sam grunted. He smoothed his hand along Jenna's arm.

Allen shrugged. "You, your wife and that purple-haired LC agent no one wants to wake up really shouldn't hang with WS. Once the LC loses control, and the Net is back up for everyone, two faces, specific imagines of a pair of newlyweds, will be plastered on screens around the world."

"They're— We're either on our own then or endangering innocents?" Kurt snapped.

Allen scowled. "Shut up." He turned back to Sam. "There's a Jeep. Older vehicle, but fast and inconspicuous. Coordinates are programmed in it. You'll have about ten minutes to exit the city, another twenty to reach

Amish country before your horse and buggy departs without you."

Sam couldn't help the wide smile breaking out on his face. Not many knew the obscure traditionalists who embraced a lifestyle with limited technology still existed. They'd be low in numbers. A quaint community surviving on small parcels of farmland without government assistance — and no threat to anyone.

"Brilliant. Thanks," Sam said.

Jenna unstuck her face from Sam's bare chest. She turned to peek toward Kurt, who was staring at the hover floor. "Kurt? You'll help carry Lav? We can't wake him because of that concussion."

Kurt jerked his chin up. "You want me to come with you?"

Sam sighed. "Hell yes." He smiled at his friend and turned to Jenna. "And hell no. We can't wake Harding because he looks like a freak. No hiding that hair beneath a top hat. And if you insist on dragging him with us, I vote he stays in the body bag indefinitely."

Jenna eased loose of his arms. She raised her hand to touch his forehead where he'd been shot. "You've a scar."

"As do you." Sam started to slide his hand into her robe, aiming for beneath her breast. She slapped his arm and he withdrew. "Fine. But remember, only your husband gets to rub that area."

"You two are either with Dexter or us," Allen told Tim, who was sitting beside Lander, holding her arm. "What'll it be?"

Tim's Adam's apple bobbed. The man had yet to get any color back in his face. "I've a wife. A son. Drop me near the A-bullet train. I have to get home. Make sure no black suits are messing with them." He released

Lander. "If I or my family goes missing, my father's a sergeant. He'll kick up a ruckus. Whereas you…"

Lander scowled. "I'm expendable. That's what you're saying? Who'll miss little ol' orphan me without a wife or husband to complain?"

"Damn right."

She punched him. Hard in the chest. His chest that certainly ached as badly as Sam's did.

The man gasped. "Hey. Not expendable — vulnerable." Tim matched Lander's frown and raised it up a notch before falling backward to lay flat.

Kurt shuffled closer, his hands filled with a pair of black pants and what looked like straps to hold them up. "Come with us," he told Lander. "Please. We need all the help we can get."

A shy smile crossed the pretty agent's face. She used her partner's chest, ignoring Tim's groan, to push off and find her feet. Short as Jenna, she could stand straight. "Since you asked so nicely. But I don't need protection, understand?" She glanced down at her rumpled brown uniform. "Where's my damn gun? My wrist phone?"

Allen rummaged through another bag. He pulled out an old-fashioned hunk of material, shades of dull brown that had to be an ankle-length dress. He threw it at Lander. "Cain's probably still smoking. You gotta stay off the grid, sister, for as long as it takes."

Lander caught the dress and laughed. "Wow. This looks…lame. Oh so lame." She unzipped her uniform, stepped out of it sporting a lacy red bra and matching panties. "I can keep my own underwear, right?"

Sam watched the other men all nod fervently. For the first time, he saw a trace of light in Kurt's eyes.

Kurt sidled closer to Lander. "Wait. Don't put that sack on yet. You said you'd help. You know how these things fit? Suspenders? I mean, seriously? And the bonnets are for Sam and Harding, not you or Jenna, right?" He tossed Sam a weak grin. "I, obviously, get not a top hat—you got that wrong—but the straw hat with the wider brim."

Sam jerked his gaze to a sight much more interesting than an agent blushing at a grieving widower as Kurt unbuttoned his formal white shirt. Sam grasped Jenna, and tugged her to stand with him. A gentle rocking, then a cessation of motion informed him they'd landed—most likely in some obscure parking lot. He didn't take his stare from his wife, not even to look as his hand shot out to catch a brown bonnet before it bopped him in the head.

# Chapter Seventeen

*Seven weeks later*

"Jenna," whispered a deep voice. "Wake up."

She blinked her eyes open, reaching for her husband...who didn't lie beside her. She sat up so fast her head snapped back.

"Shh, dearie, it's just me." Lav grinned down at her, looking as if he'd swallowed an entire flock of canaries. "I've news. Wonderful news. Trouble should be on the way. There's this guy who'll guide by plane, then Jeep, then horseback."

"Your boyfriend's coming?"

"I hope so." Lav winked. "And I do mean to both here and in my bed. If he feels welcome, I know he'll say yes to more than a visit."

"Where's Sam?"

Lav snorted and lost his doting smile. "Your man— that man—is so irritating. It's been almost two months since H-day, hiding out in one strange place after another, until this cabin in the mountains which I actually love. It's so quaint. But the prickly dolt who thinks he's king of this cute little nest still won't take a walk with me, let alone let me shave that ugly face or cut his hair. *Everyone* loves me. So why does *he* hate me?"

"H-day?" she asked.

"Yeah. Kurt said it's what everyone's calling the day honeymoons became as obsolete and deadly as marriage can be. Jenna, what'd I ever do but take a bullet for him? Twice?"

"Ha. That first bullet had *your* name on it, not mine," Sam called from the doorway. "Get away from my...Jesus, nude wife, you bastard."

Jenna yanked the sheet up to her chin.

Lav scowled. "Nothing I haven't seen before."

"Did I hear right? You've someone taking you out of here by horse, Jeep and *plane*?" Sam stomped closer and slapped Lav on the back. "Didn't think you had the balls to get in the sky again. Leaving soon? This morning?" Sam exaggerated his eager smile and Jenna scowled at him.

"No," she said. "We weren't talking about anyone leaving. It's not safe. Not until we get a better set of identities in a new city."

"Cities, right?" Sam quipped.

Lav snorted. "As if I haven't had enough of you too, dearie. Not like I asked to be kidnapped by a blogger turned terrorist, held and tortured until I gave testimony for and against ex-co-workers over and over until I threw up, and on the run farther and farther from my friends and my life."

"Tortured? Ha. I'm the one subjected to the constant whining. And, pretty boy, there's no time for walks. You could work the garden, help repair the far wall, do anything but cook and complain and never wash a single dish."

"You *love* my cooking. Fine. Asshole. I'll break my nails on manual labor, instead of tapping away, tweaking signals and wrist phones so you can blog without pissing away our locale or getting Cained." Lav chuckled. "Get it? Fried like the guy I never met. I just laid about in his home almost dead, while the rest of you hatched the dumbest plan ever. Anyway — on topic — you're too stupid to understand simple bounces using mere thousands of satellites…"

Jenna tuned the pair out, pressing her face against the pillow and wondering why she felt so tired. The glow of terror from H-day had long faded with the bliss of night after night sleeping and waking in Sam's arms, but this morning found her again with her bones aching as if she'd parachuted yesterday. Maybe because the repercussions, ripples and effects continued without an end in sight. Or could something more parasitic and permanent than worldly troubles be draining away at her? How wondrous and perfect would that be?

*Stop. Don't even think it to yourself or you'll jinx paradise.*

Despite the weight of eight billion humans, the world still turned, but it'd shifted on its axis with confusion and the persistent threat of more chaos flaring up. Considerably more time and resources, by hopefully honest authorities, were needed to sort out the politics of leaders worldwide being indicted, processed and charged or not, while underlings stepped up to prove they could govern with more integrity than their bosses.

The sudden silence between the bickering men she'd come to love as thoroughly as a human could another — more than life itself — drew her attention to the one who melted her into a lump of lust every time she looked at him, which was as often as possible while awake and consistently in her dreams. That darkening in Sam's deep green eyes wasn't good. She sighed as he shoved his hand into his hip pocket and pulled out...a switchblade?

Large violet eyes went huge and Lav's Adam's apple bobbed.

"Sam. Leave his hair alone," she snapped.

"But..."

"No buts. If he doesn't want to cut it, he doesn't want to cut it."

Sam slumped and retracted the blade. "Yes, dear."

"Hey. I call her dear, not you." Lav dropped his chin, hiding his face with his hair. "And...Dexter, you're serious? Really want me to leave?"

"Hell yes. I hate picking purple hair out of the shower. Instead of dragging some other long-haired freak here—this unnamed friend of yours—why don't you go visit? Move in with him?"

Lav bristled. "You know Charlie's secret code name's Trouble. And his hair's shorter than yours. He's beautiful, so strong and going to karate chop your ass the moment he hears how mean you are to me."

"Charlie?" Sam grinned. "As in Charles Ricker? I suspected but really find it hard to believe that the famous actor who stars in all those remakes of Bruce Lee movies actually likes *you*."

Lav slapped his fingers over his mouth. "Oops. No, no. My man, named Trouble, isn't some celebrity whom you'll draw into your spiderweb—this online and offline, deadly battle with the peons of corrupt admirals lurking everywhere."

Jenna hid her shudder. Yesterday numerous commenters on the blog said authorities had arrested a man, Gary Fenton whom she'd known intimately, who'd survived his honeymoon. He was charged with fraud, seeing as his twin brother, not him, was the applicant registered with the LC. Fenton cut a deal, claimed he could lead them to Thomas Madison, the agent who'd played the role of medic and done his best to see Lav dead. Yet another reason to keep Lav close, until Thomas joined Admiral Keltz behind bars.

"If the world learns," Lav snapped at Sam, "Trouble is considering joining the notorious *Out of the Loop* asshat, he won't seriously think about pretending to be on indefinite hiatus to Tibet or Timbuktu or anywhere. He'll never give up the attention to hang with me in Nowhere Land until the world's declared free of tyranny. And that'll never happen, so yeah, I should go home where at least I can hold someone who loves me before I'm shot. Again. Then my man—who isn't a selfish prick—would try to rescue me and eat a ton of bullets." Lav wilted, giving them a glimpse of a woebegone expression before he turned aside.

Her brows arched and she looked to Sam. He rolled his eyes before he moved to fling his arm around Lav, whose gaze went wary with surprise.

"Maybe if you cut that damn hair, he'd be here already and stay as long as he wants," Sam muttered.

Lav blinked and pulled back. "But...I told him not to uproot because you want me to cut the hair he loves and leave Jenna and you and never follow or see you again."

"I never said that. And, you insecure phony, don't you think he should like you for you? What type of jerk stays with someone because he..." Sam grasped a fistful of Lav's hair, thrusting it aside. "Christ, stop me now. I don't want to even imagine what you two do with all this hair."

Lav leaned to smack a kiss on Sam's forehead. "You want me around, the best uncle in the world?"

*Uncle? Huh?*

"Sure," Sam mumbled, pushing Lav away and stepping back.

"You really do love me?"

"Whatever." Sam raised his clenched fist. "Get the hell out of my bedroom before I show you how much."

Lav's eyes gleamed. He winked at Jenna. "See you in ten, dearie. Someday, your lazy man will let me show him how to last…" Lav gulped at the look on Sam's face and ran. He made it to the threshold of the door before the closed switchblade Sam threw smacked him in the back. Not an idiot, Lav bent to pick up the knife and bolted.

Sam stomped after him and slammed the door closed. He turned, dark eyes smoldering, as he stared at her smiling at him. "You complained to him? Ten minutes? Seriously?"

Jenna laughed. "Of course not. I told him I can't last five minutes and he changed it to you and ten. But you can prove me right, as always, at least twice before I get up. I don't know why I slept so long." *Oh God.* Maybe she did. She was never late — not ever.

Sam closed in. He flung himself down on the bed beside her. "You know I like teasing him, right? I don't know how I survived before without you, the freak, Kurt and Lander in my life. I like it here. I want to put up that picket fence, a dog house for Lav and a nearby cabin for Kurt and Lander after he figures out how long he needs to grieve and they start doing more than occasionally brushing shoulders."

Jenna smiled, her heart soaring. If only Sam was ready to accept one more person into their circle. "I still don't know why Kurt and Lander went on a supply run when we're not low on anything important. You hear from them?"

"Yeah. Should be back in a few hours." Sam reached to rest his hand on her stomach. "And yes, they did go after some…"

The sound of rapidly approaching footsteps caused Sam to stiffen. He sat up.

Lav burst into the room without a call out or knocking.

"Damn it," Sam snarled. "Man, you're so asking for a beat—Lav? What the hell you'd do?"

Jenna sat up, clutching the sheet to her chest. Her jaw dropped.

Lav's hair barely reached his shoulders, chopped off like he'd taken that switchblade to it. He stood facing them, tears springing into his eyes. "You gotta help me, Jenna. He…Charlie is… Sam, that note from Kurt in your messages is true? Charlie is on his way with him and Lander and they'll be here…" Lav gasped. "This morning, not tonight?"

Sam lunged from the bed to stand with arms crossed. "You broke my codes? Read my mail?"

"Of course. I did the first week here. Jenna…my hair. I cut it before I read his"—Lav jerked his thumb at Sam—"mail. Thought I had all day. It makes sense if I remain hiding out with you I'm not so easily identified. I can't—won't—ever do anything to put you in jeopardy. Pleeease. Get your lazy pregnant ass out of bed and make me beautiful. It's only fair you help…Jenna? Whaaat? You didn't know we all know?"

*Oh my God, I'm really pregnant?*

"Get out," roared Sam.

Lav remained rooted to the floor. He tugged at the ends of his hair. "Sam, what'll I do? I look terrible, right?"

Sam sighed. "Leave my wife alone. I'll help in…" he grinned, "ten. I heard a famous actor pulled out most of his hair shortly after the LC witch hunt on employees. Worried about some vain guy who could now surprise him by being nearly as bald as he is."

*I'm gonna have a baby?*

Lav lit up, eyes twinkling like a nuclear bomb went off inside his head. "'K. That's a good idea. But seeing as it's *your* idea, I'll stick to my plan of dyeing what's left orange — or blue." He twisted for the door, pivoting to blow them a kiss. "I love you both."

"Jesus, kill me now," Sam grumbled. He sat heavily on the edge of the bed and pushed back to his feet as Lav exited. "And he doesn't even close the damn door." He stomped, slammed the door closed, and paused. He crossed the room and grabbed a chair.

"I'm having...a...baby?"

Sam strode to wedge the chair beneath the doorknob and turned. His eyes shone so bright, a supernova had to have detonated. "No."

"Oh." Her chin fell, taking her heart with it. But surely that was for the best. Sam didn't honestly want a kid, not living in hiding like this.

The bed dipped beside her and a strong finger forced her chin up. "You're not having a baby. *We* are. You and me. Husband and wife."

Her lungs froze. "Really? How do you know?"

Sam scowled. "I wanted to tell you. I wanted you to tell me."

"But how?"

"Lavender Harding, the friend of yours I'm gonna kill, said your breasts looked swollen. I asked Lander to pick up one of those new bloodtest kits." Sam had the decency to blush. "I didn't want you to think I was behaving badly, worried about things, especially if that demented freak was staring at your breasts without reason and I blackened both his eyes. Even more important, why torture my needle-phobic girl? So I drew some blood after you'd fallen asleep. You'll be glad to know you test healthy for diseases other than pregnancy."

"You stuck a needle in me and I didn't wake up? When?"

"Last week." Sam stroked his fingers up her arm and tugged down the sheet. "The night you had me beneath you, then behind you." Propped on his elbow, he drew little circles on her chest. "That's the reason for this supply run." Bursts of excitement fanned out through her as he inched his fingers up, widening then tightening his path to include her breast. "Prenatal vitamins, portable sonogram machine, backup battery for the Jeep and routes tested for the closest medical center are on the way." He stared down at her, love and hope spreading across his face. "You're happy? Want my baby?"

She smiled back with all her heart. "No."

He narrowed his eyes, his hand on her breast gone still.

"I want *our* baby."

He chuckled and lowered his palm to rest on her belly. "Right, beautiful mommy-to-be. Why don't you sleep some more, while I go strangle the nuisance who woke you both up?"

"I don't think so. I've no memory of this night last week," she lied. "You have to show me how you made me pass out so thoroughly I didn't feel the little prick of a needle." *Just the big one of my awesome husband. My husband. How I love those two words.*

Sam rolled to his feet. In less than a second, his clothes lay on the floor. She squealed as his powerful hands tore away the sheet, grabbed and lifted her. Sam threw himself on his back and pulled her down over him. "As you wish. But, sweetheart, how are you gonna know what I do after you faint from that much loving?"

She laughed as he clasped her butt, guiding her to crouch over his delicious, rising erection, her knees clamped against his hips. "Get real. You're the one who's gonna pass out this time."

He reared up, arms wrapped around her and mouth homing in. He paused an inch away from her. "How about we stick together, awake and passed out, always and forever."

"Sealed with a —"

His lips took hers and Jenna knew happiness, from head to toe.

# About the Author

Sci-fi, paranormal, thriller-mystery, indefinable—I'm an author who adds sweet and spicy layers of romance to any genre.

I was born in upstate New York, USA, land of cows, snow, drizzle and sometimes a ray of sun. I spent my childhood reading whatever I could get my hands on. Adolescence found me questioning the validity of everything I read. Early twenties, I headed for the Pacific Ocean. A stop off to visit a friend turned into years in Tucson, Arizona. My late twenties found me running family owned greenhouses and florist shops back in New York. When the reality of retail life became too mundane to handle, I began an obsessive love of creating more interesting worlds.

Arlene Webb loves to hear from readers. You can find her contact information, website and author biography at http://www.totallybound.com.

Home of Erotic Romance